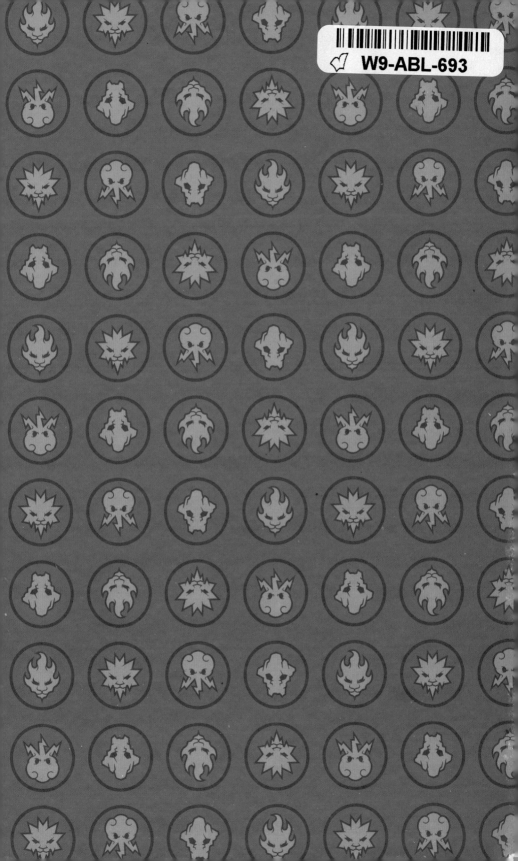

LEGO NINJAGO
Masters of Spinjitzu

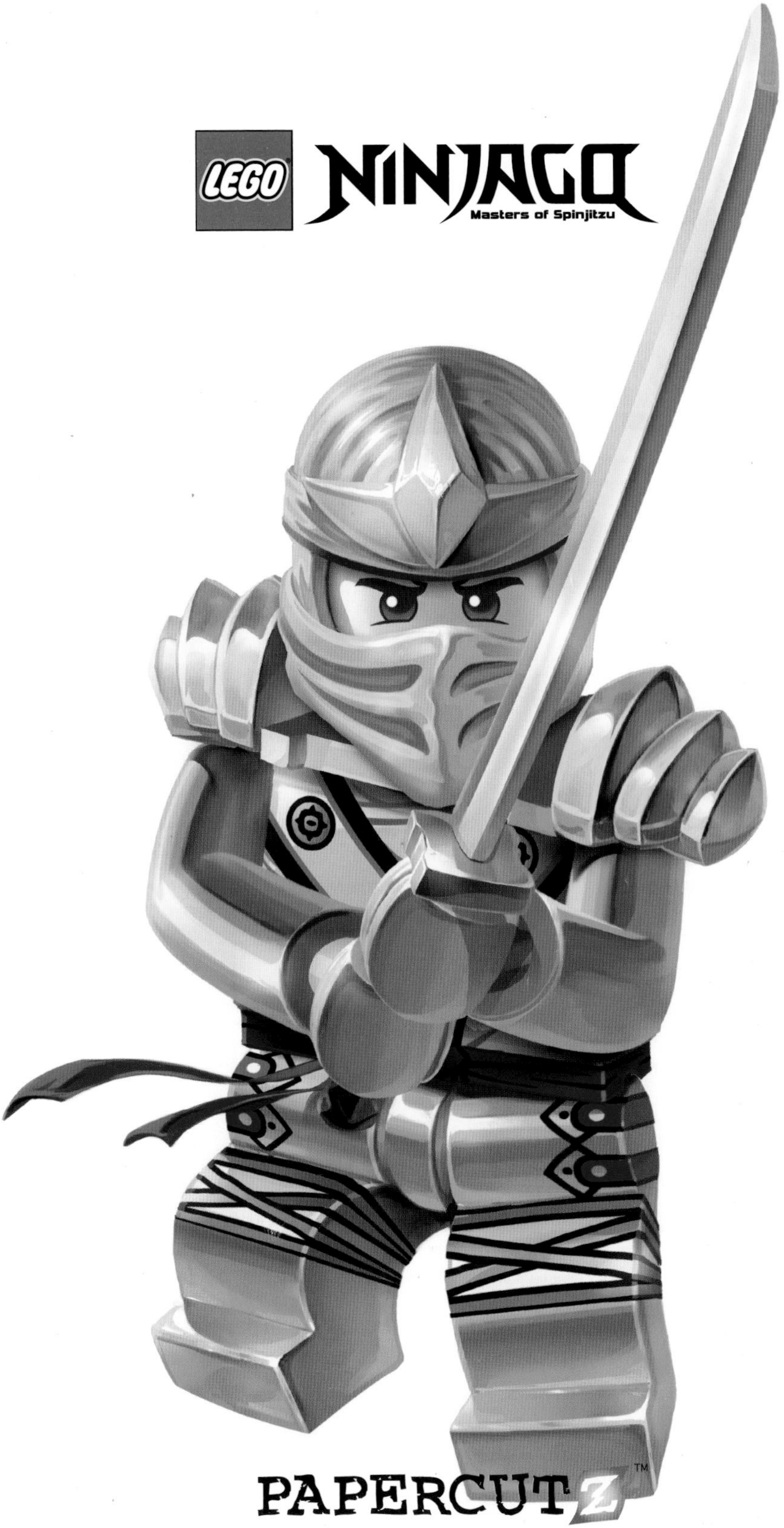

PAPERCUTZ™

LEGO® GRAPHIC NOVELS AVAILABLE FROM PAPERCUTZ

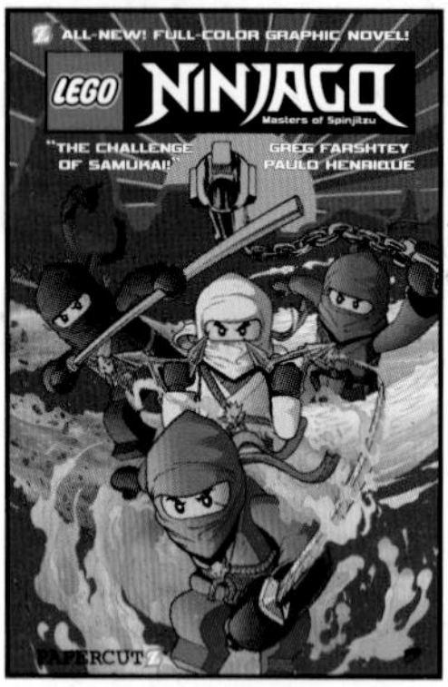
ALL-NEW! FULL-COLOR GRAPHIC NOVEL!
LEGO NINJAGO
Masters of Spinjitzu
"THE CHALLENGE OF SAMUKAI!"
GREG FARSHTEY
PAULO HENRIQUE
PAPERCUTZ

LEGO NINJAGO #1

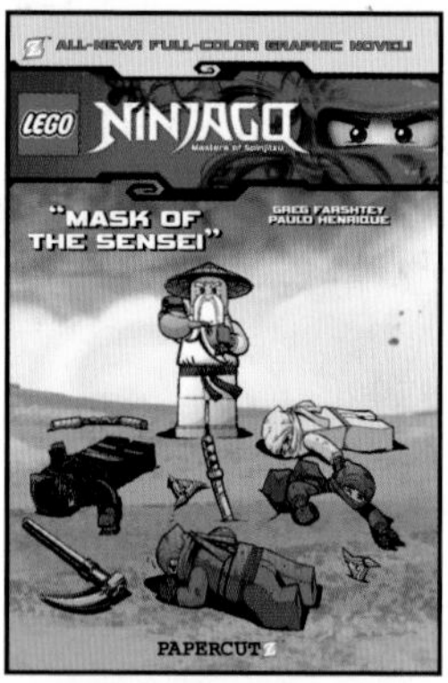
ALL-NEW! FULL-COLOR GRAPHIC NOVEL!
LEGO NINJAGO
"MASK OF THE SENSEI"
GREG FARSHTEY
PAULO HENRIQUE
PAPERCUTZ

LEGO NINJAGO #2

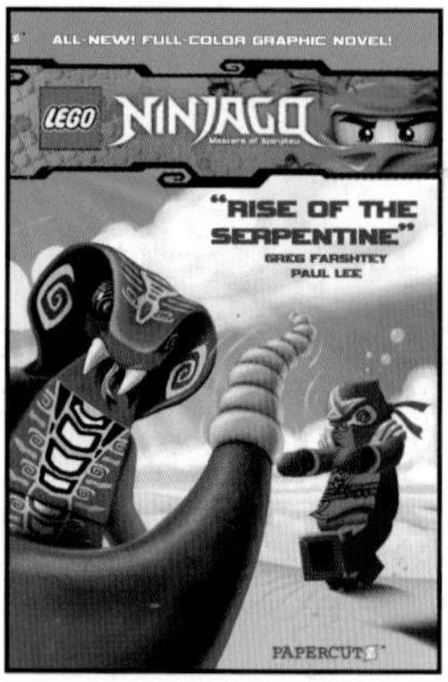
ALL-NEW! FULL-COLOR GRAPHIC NOVEL!
LEGO NINJAGO
"RISE OF THE SERPENTINE"
GREG FARSHTEY
PAUL LEE
PAPERCUTZ

LEGO NINJAGO #3

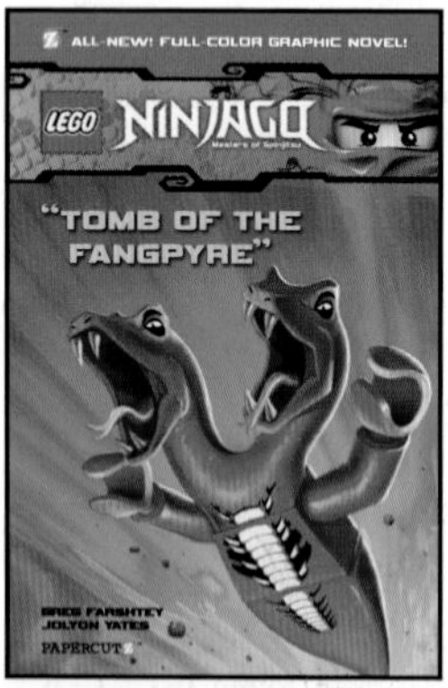
ALL-NEW! FULL-COLOR GRAPHIC NOVEL!
LEGO NINJAGO
"TOMB OF THE FANGPYRE"
GREG FARSHTEY
JOLYON YATES
PAPERCUTZ

LEGO NINJAGO #4

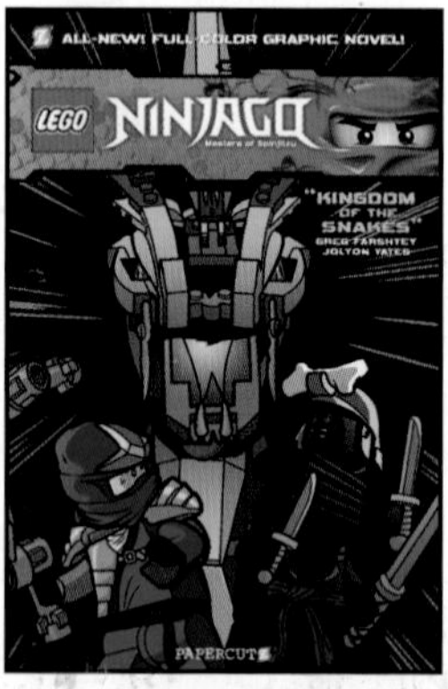
ALL-NEW! FULL-COLOR GRAPHIC NOVEL!
LEGO NINJAGO
"KINGDOM OF THE SNAKES"
GREG FARSHTEY
JOLYON YATES
PAPERCUTZ

LEGO NINJAGO #5

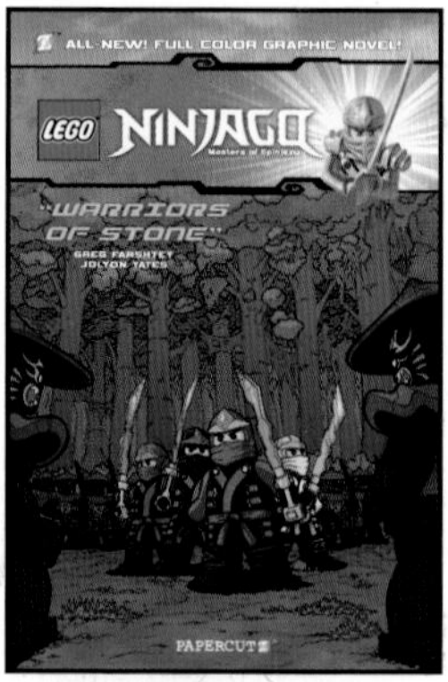
ALL-NEW! FULL-COLOR GRAPHIC NOVEL!
LEGO NINJAGO
"WARRIORS OF STONE"
GREG FARSHTEY
JOLYON YATES
PAPERCUTZ

LEGO NINJAGO #6

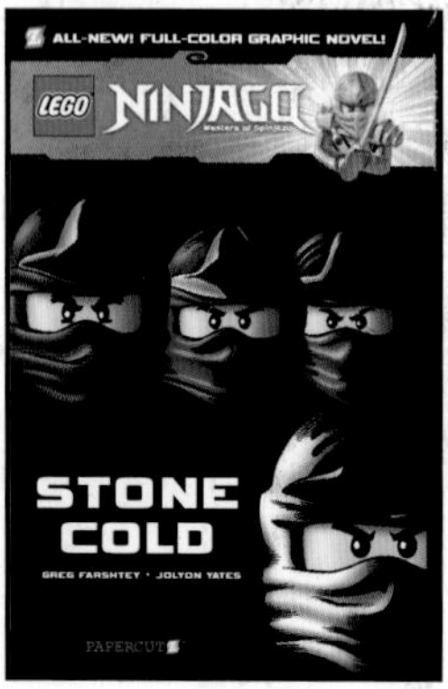
ALL-NEW! FULL-COLOR GRAPHIC NOVEL!
LEGO NINJAGO
STONE COLD
GREG FARSHTEY • JOLYON YATES
PAPERCUTZ

LEGO NINJAGO #7

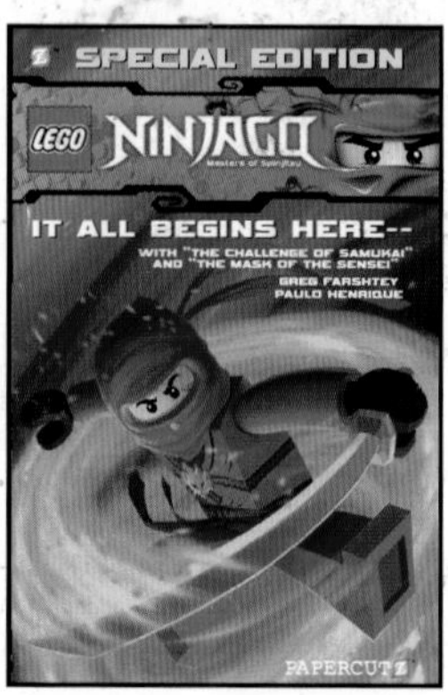
SPECIAL EDITION
LEGO NINJAGO
IT ALL BEGINS HERE--
WITH "THE CHALLENGE OF SAMUKAI" AND "THE MASK OF THE SENSEI"
GREG FARSHTEY
PAULO HENRIQUE
PAPERCUTZ

LEGO NINJAGO SPECIAL EDITION #1
(Features stories from NINJAGO #1 and #2.)

COMING SOON!

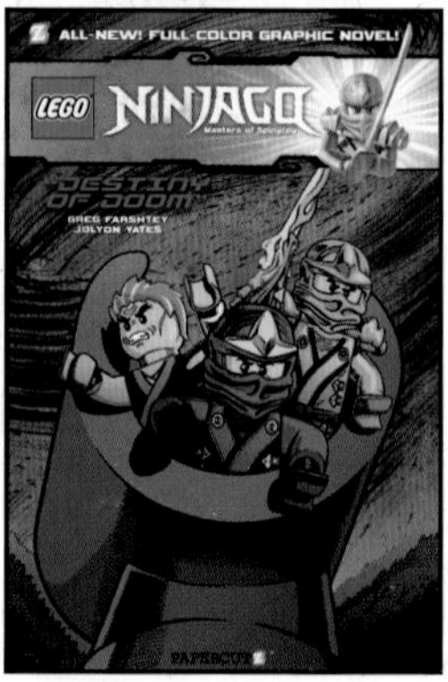
ALL-NEW! FULL-COLOR GRAPHIC NOVEL!
LEGO NINJAGO
"DESTINY OF DOOM"
GREG FARSHTEY
JOLYON YATES
PAPERCUTZ

LEGO NINJAGO #8

LEGO® NINJAGO graphic novels are available in paperback and hardcover at booksellers everywhere.

LEGO® NINJAGO #1-6 are $6.99 in paperback, and $10.99 in hardcover. LEGO NINJAGO SPECIAL EDITION #1 is $10.99 in paperback only. You can also order online at www.papercutz.com. Or call 1-800-886-1223, Monday through Friday, 9 – 5 EST. MC, Visa, and AmEx accepted. To order by mail, please add $4.00 for postage and handling for first book ordered, $1.00 for each additional book and make check payable to NBM Publishing. Send to: Papercutz, 160 Broadway, Suite 700, East Wing, New York, NY 10038.

LEGO NINJAGO graphic novels are also available digitally wherever e-books are sold.

LEGO NINJAGO

Masters of Spinjitzu

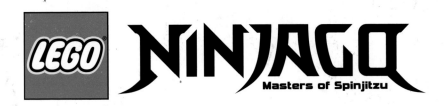

"WARRIORS OF STONE"

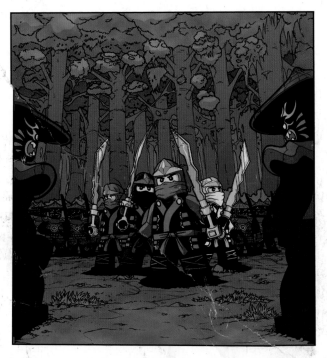

Greg Farshtey – Writer

Jolyon Yates – Artist

Jayjay Jackson – Colorist

Paulo Henrique – Cover Artist

Laurie E. Smith – Cover Colorist

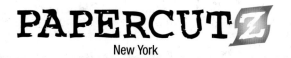

PAPERCUTZ

New York

LEGO® NINJAGO Masters of Spinjitzu
#6 "Warriors of Stone"

GREG FARSHTEY – Writer
JOLYON YATES – Artist
JAYJAY JACKSON – Colorist
BRYAN SENKA – Letterer
Production by NELSON DESIGN GROUP, LLC
Associate Editor – MICHAEL PETRANEK
JIM SALICRUP
Editor-in-Chief

ISBN: 978-1-59707-378-3 paperback edition
ISBN: 978-1-59707-379-0 hardcover edition

Papercutz books may be purchased for business or promotional use. For information on bulk purchases please contact Macmillan Corporate and Premium Sales Department at (800) 221-7945 x5442.

Printed in China
August 2013 by Asia One Printing, LTD
13/F Asia One Tower
8 Fung Yip St., Chaiwan, Hong Kong

Distributed by Macmillan

Second Printing

FSC
www.fsc.org
MIX
Paper from
responsible sources
FSC® C006398

MEET THE MASTERS
OF SPINJITZU...

JAY

COLE

ZANE

KAI

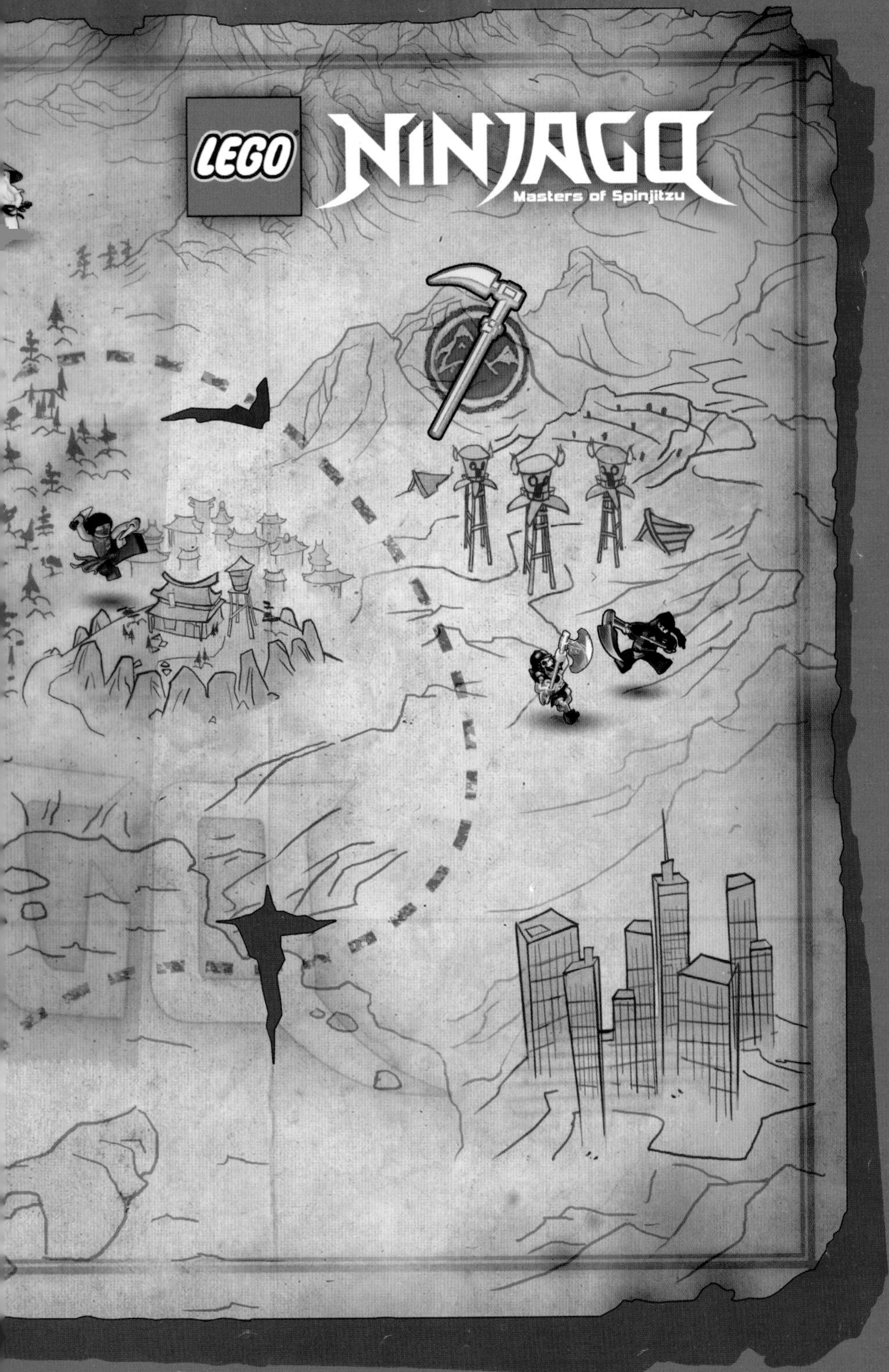
LEGO
NINJAGO
Masters of Spinjitzu

And the Master of the Masters of Spinjitzu...

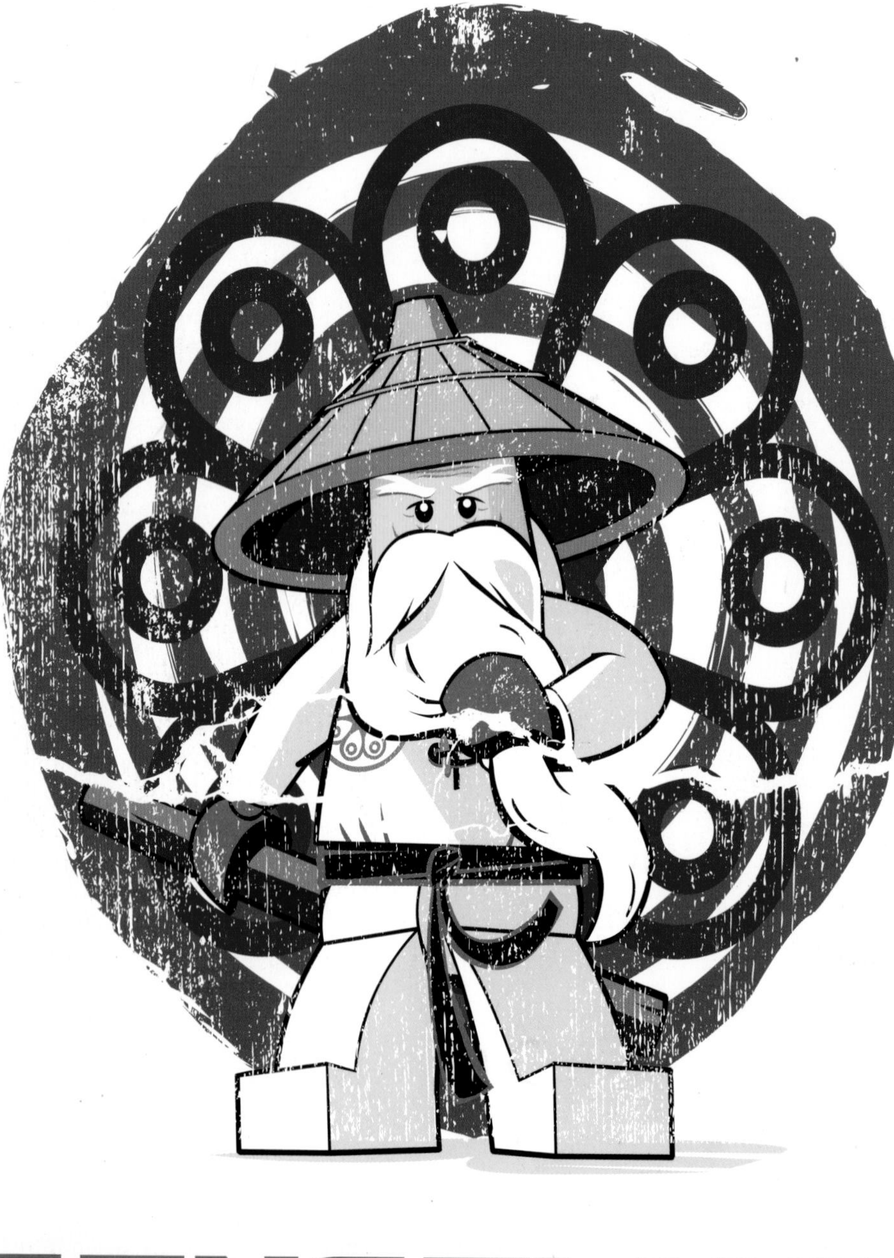

SENSEI WU

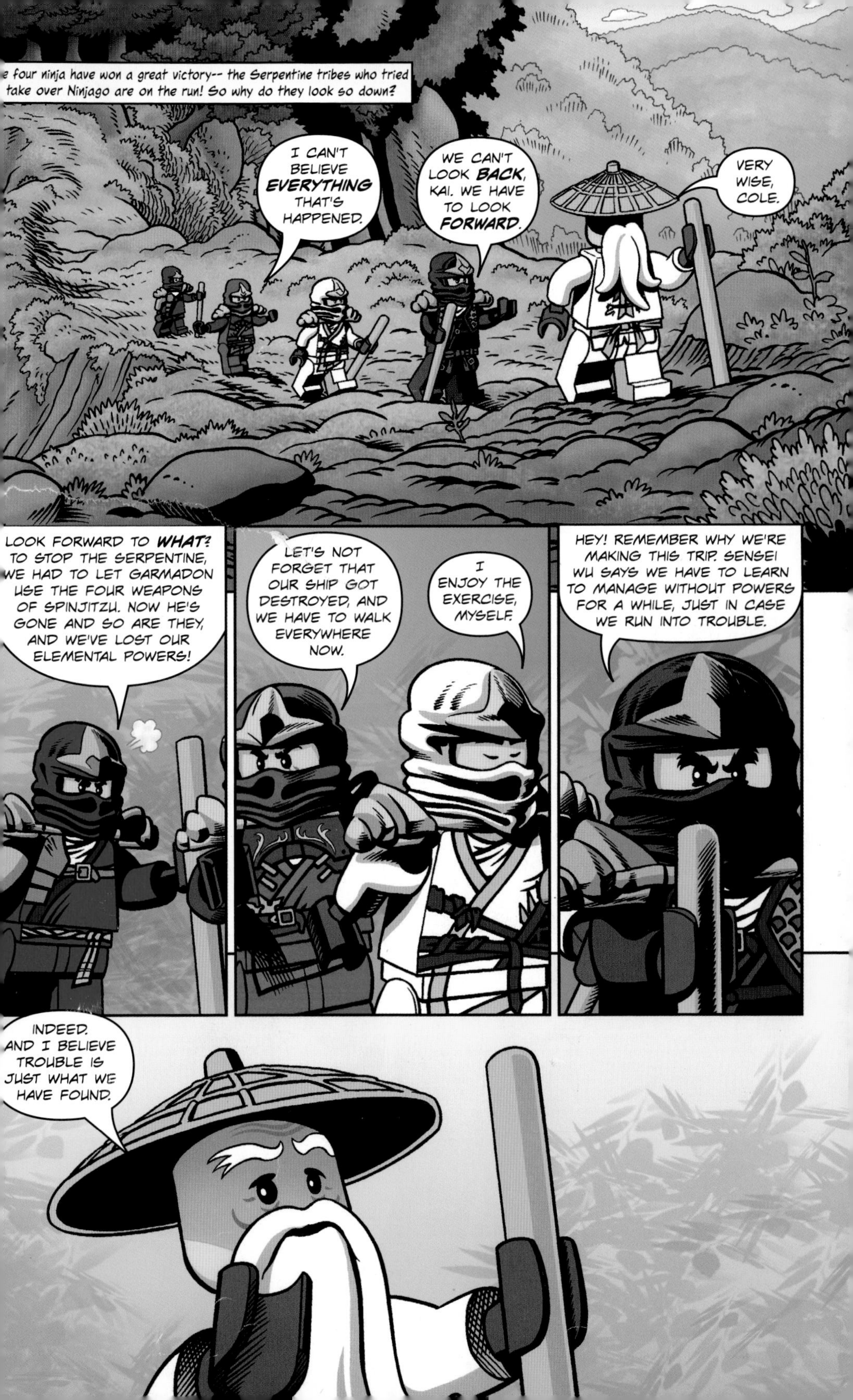
e four ninja have won a great victory-- the Serpentine tribes who tried take over Ninjago are on the run! So why do they look so down?
I CAN'T BELIEVE EVERYTHING THAT'S HAPPENED.
WE CAN'T LOOK BACK, KAI. WE HAVE TO LOOK FORWARD.
VERY WISE, COLE.
LOOK FORWARD TO WHAT? TO STOP THE SERPENTINE, WE HAD TO LET GARMADON USE THE FOUR WEAPONS OF SPINJITZU. NOW HE'S GONE AND SO ARE THEY, AND WE'VE LOST OUR ELEMENTAL POWERS!
LET'S NOT FORGET THAT OUR SHIP GOT DESTROYED, AND WE HAVE TO WALK EVERYWHERE NOW.
I ENJOY THE EXERCISE, MYSELF.
HEY! REMEMBER WHY WE'RE MAKING THIS TRIP. SENSEI WU SAYS WE HAVE TO LEARN TO MANAGE WITHOUT POWERS FOR A WHILE, JUST IN CASE WE RUN INTO TROUBLE.
INDEED. AND I BELIEVE TROUBLE IS JUST WHAT WE HAVE FOUND.

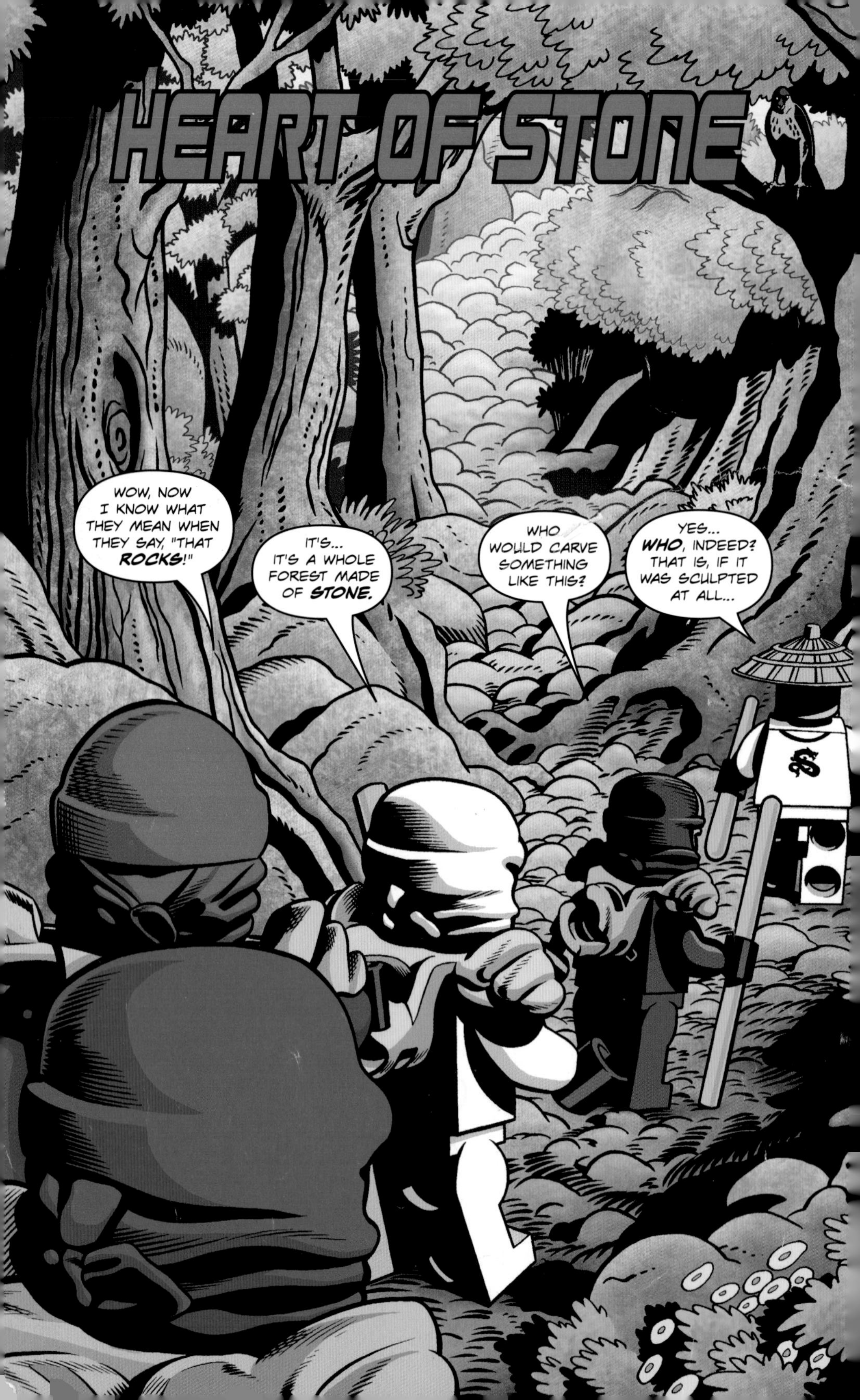
HEART OF STONE
WOW, NOW I KNOW WHAT THEY MEAN WHEN THEY SAY, "THAT ROCKS!"
IT'S... IT'S A WHOLE FOREST MADE OF STONE.
WHO WOULD CARVE SOMETHING LIKE THIS?
YES... WHO, INDEED? THAT IS, IF IT WAS SCULPTED AT ALL...

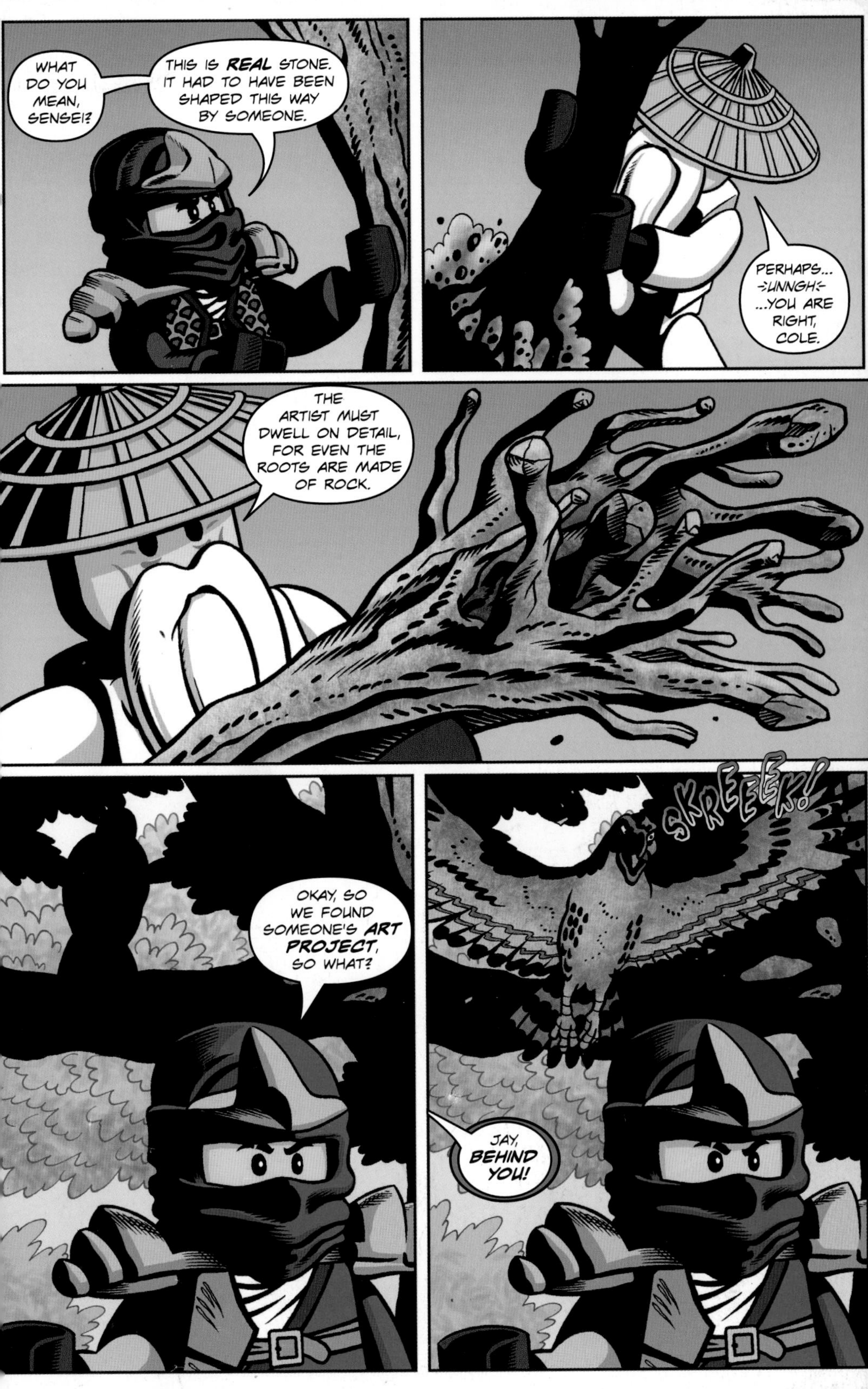

WHAT DO YOU MEAN, SENSEI?
THIS IS **REAL** STONE. IT HAD TO HAVE BEEN SHAPED THIS WAY BY SOMEONE.
PERHAPS... -UNNGH- ...YOU ARE RIGHT, COLE.
THE ARTIST MUST DWELL ON DETAIL, FOR EVEN THE ROOTS ARE MADE OF ROCK.
OKAY, SO WE FOUND SOMEONE'S **ART PROJECT**, SO WHAT?
SKREEEEK!
JAY, **BEHIND YOU!**

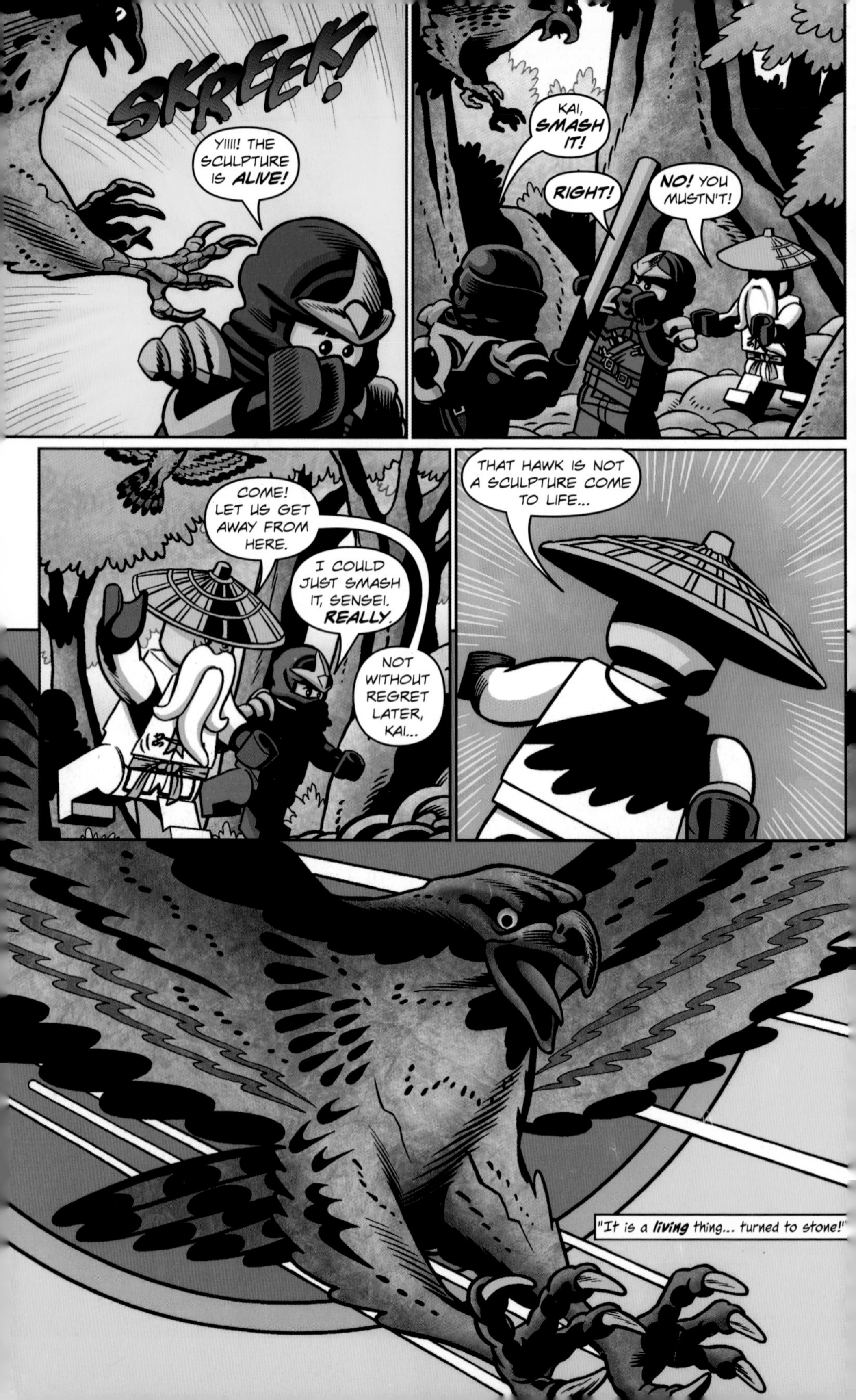
SKREEK!
YIIII! THE SCULPTURE IS ALIVE!
KAI, SMASH IT!
RIGHT!
NO! YOU MUSTN'T!
COME! LET US GET AWAY FROM HERE.
I COULD JUST SMASH IT, SENSEI. REALLY.
NOT WITHOUT REGRET LATER, KAI...
THAT HAWK IS NOT A SCULPTURE COME TO LIFE...
"It is a living thing... turned to stone!"

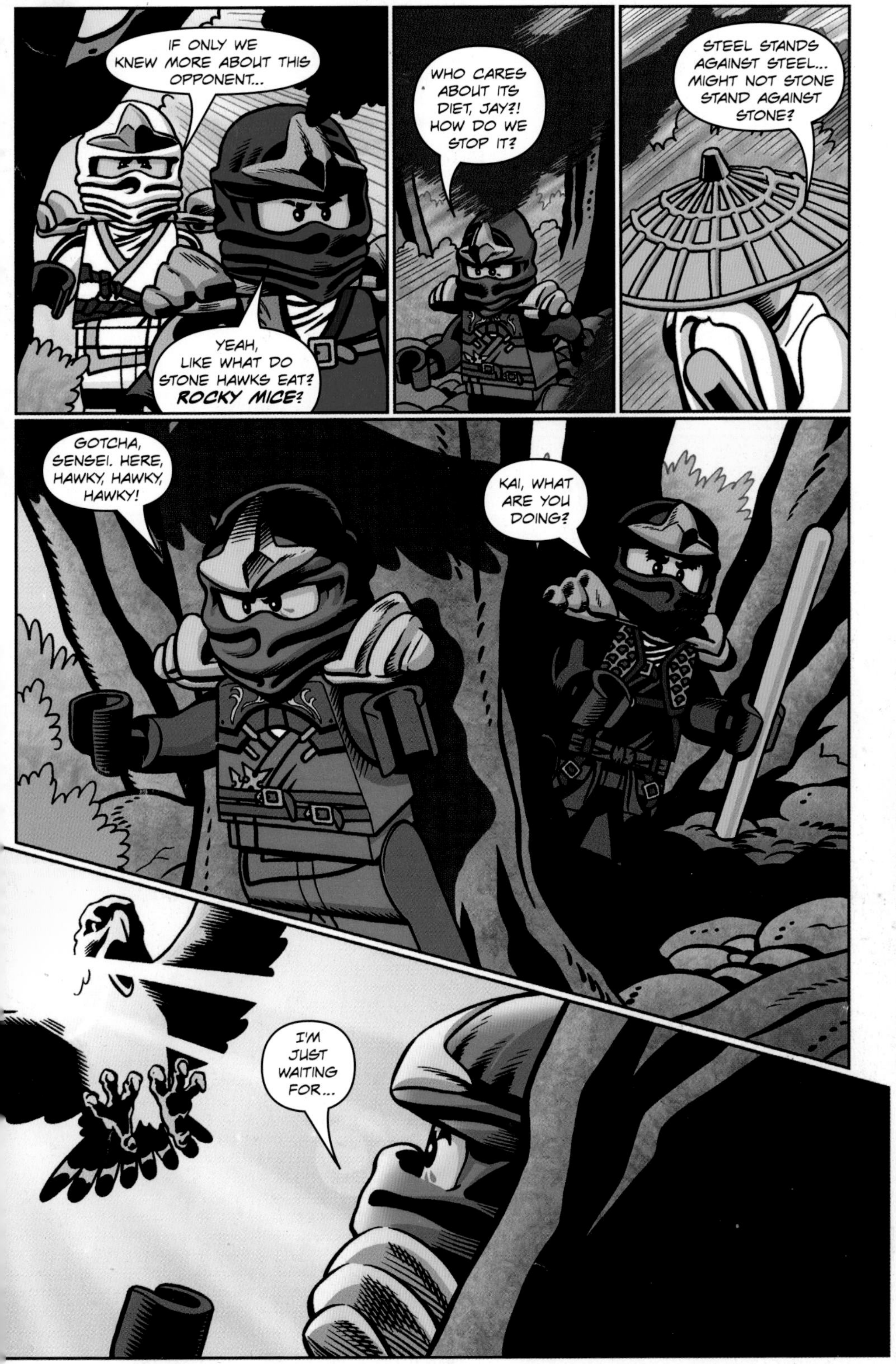
IF ONLY WE KNEW MORE ABOUT THIS OPPONENT...
YEAH, LIKE WHAT DO STONE HAWKS EAT? ROCKY MICE?
WHO CARES ABOUT ITS DIET, JAY?! HOW DO WE STOP IT?
STEEL STANDS AGAINST STEEL... MIGHT NOT STONE STAND AGAINST STONE?
GOTCHA, SENSEI. HERE, HAWKY, HAWKY, HAWKY!
KAI, WHAT ARE YOU DOING?
I'M JUST WAITING FOR...

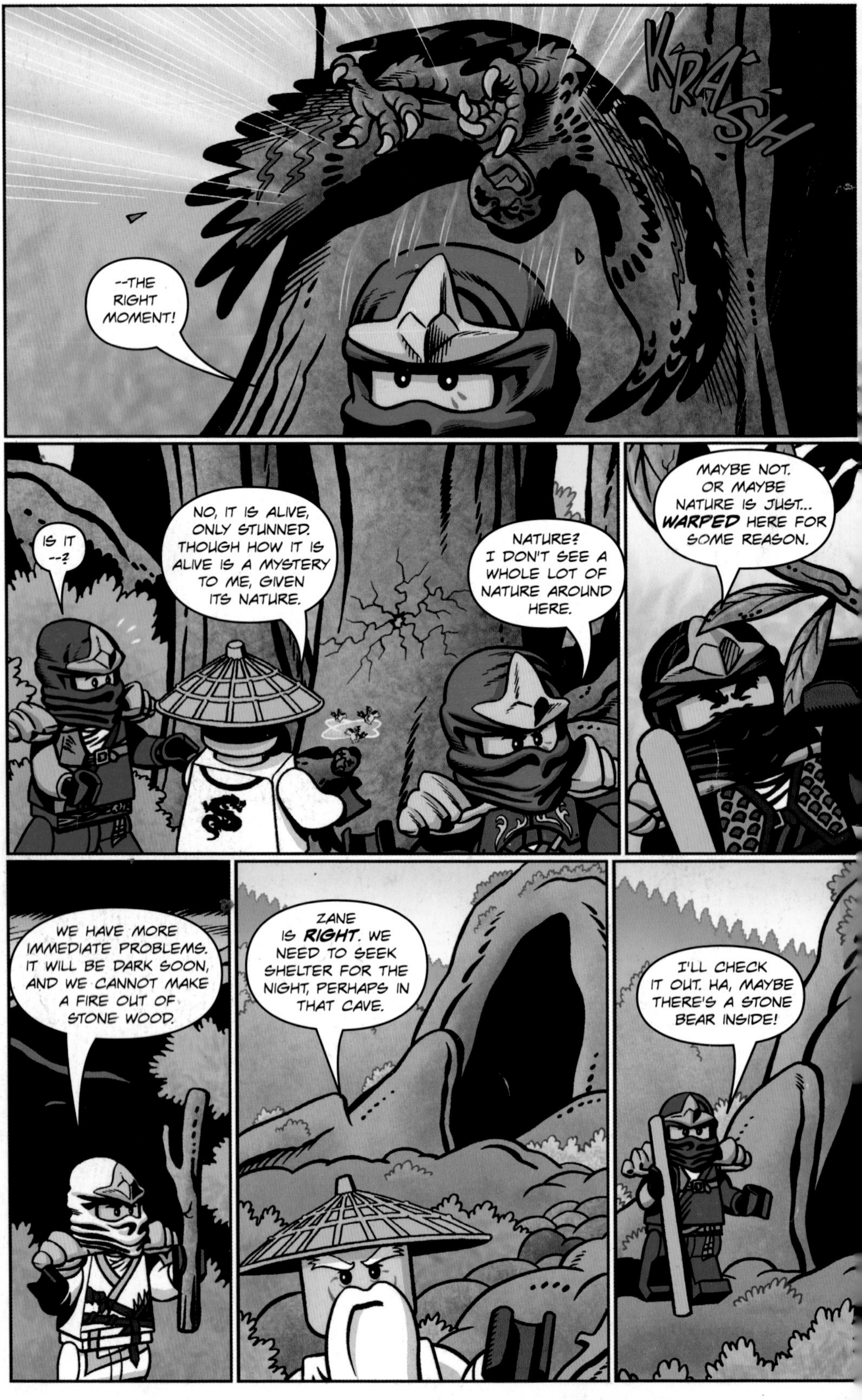
K-RA-SH
--THE RIGHT MOMENT!
IS IT --?
NO, IT IS ALIVE, ONLY STUNNED. THOUGH HOW IT IS ALIVE IS A MYSTERY TO ME, GIVEN ITS NATURE.
NATURE? I DON'T SEE A WHOLE LOT OF NATURE AROUND HERE.
MAYBE NOT. OR MAYBE NATURE IS JUST... **WARPED** HERE FOR SOME REASON.
WE HAVE MORE IMMEDIATE PROBLEMS. IT WILL BE DARK SOON, AND WE CANNOT MAKE A FIRE OUT OF STONE WOOD.
ZANE IS **RIGHT**. WE NEED TO SEEK SHELTER FOR THE NIGHT, PERHAPS IN THAT CAVE.
I'LL CHECK IT OUT. HA, MAYBE THERE'S A STONE BEAR INSIDE!

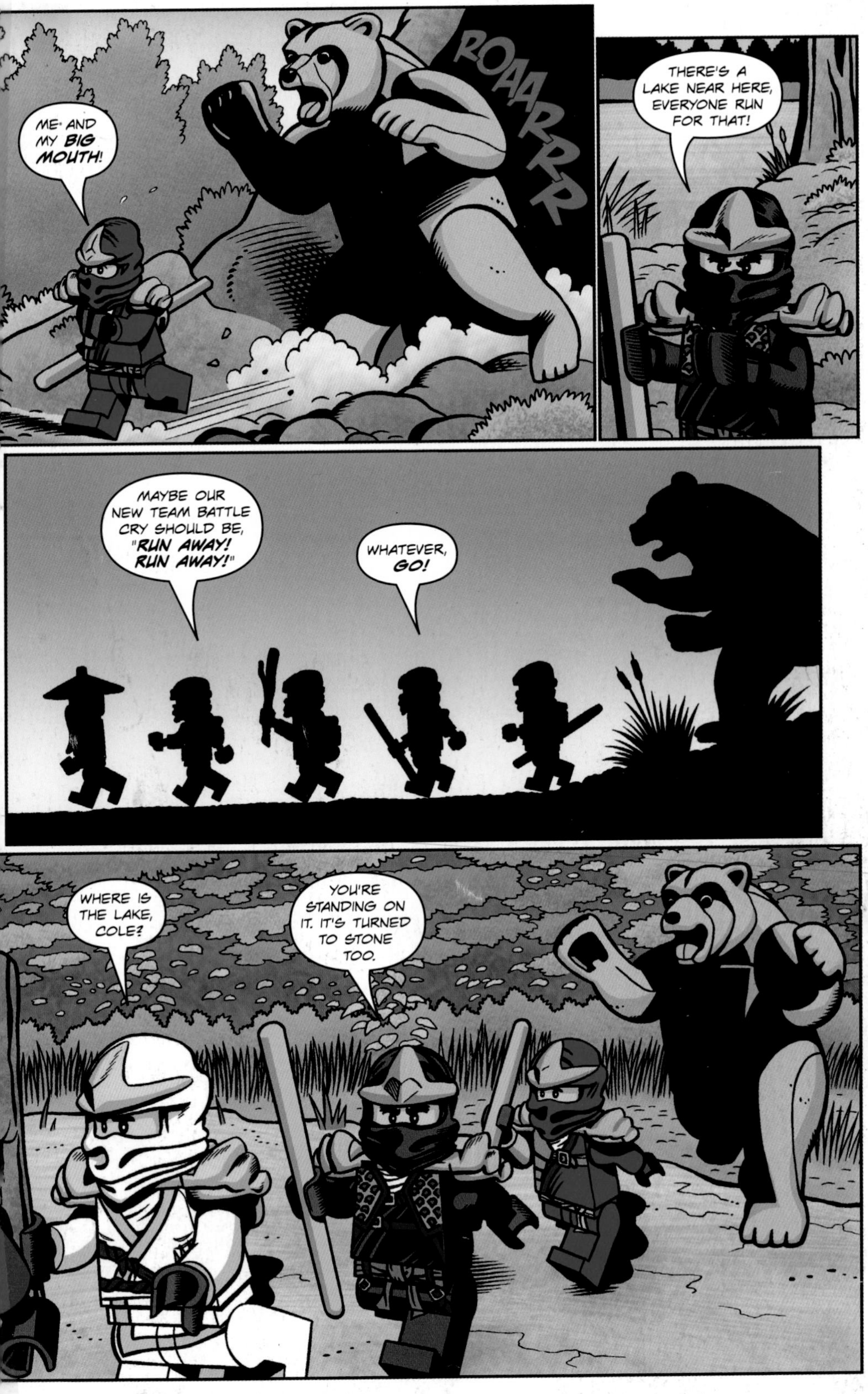
ME AND MY **BIG MOUTH!**
ROAAARRR
THERE'S A LAKE NEAR HERE, EVERYONE RUN FOR THAT!
MAYBE OUR NEW TEAM BATTLE CRY SHOULD BE, "**RUN AWAY! RUN AWAY!**"
WHATEVER, **GO!**
WHERE IS THE LAKE, COLE?
YOU'RE STANDING ON IT. IT'S TURNED TO STONE TOO.

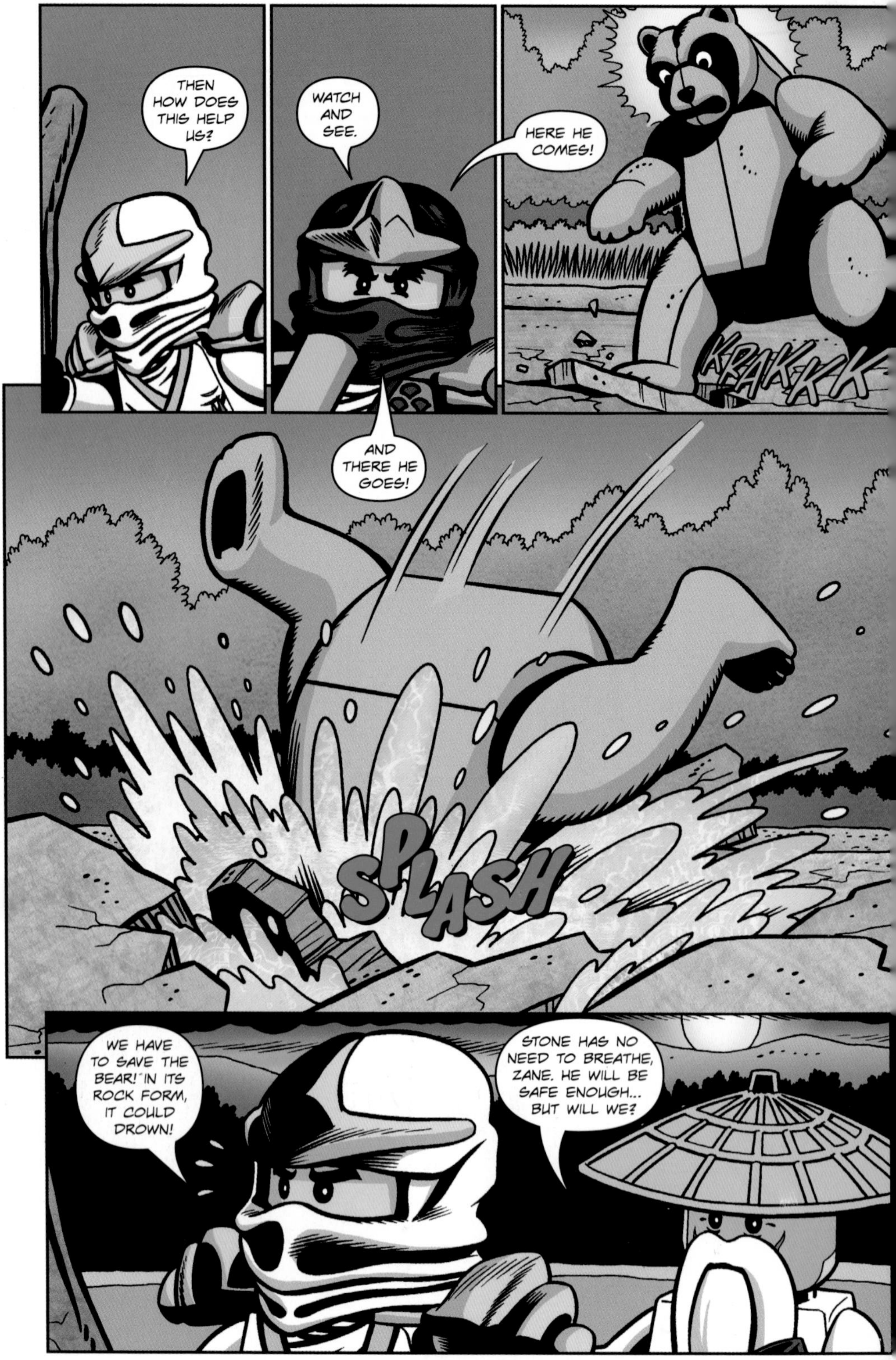
THEN HOW DOES THIS HELP US?
WATCH AND SEE.
HERE HE COMES!
KRAKKKK
AND THERE HE GOES!
SPLASH
WE HAVE TO SAVE THE BEAR! IN ITS ROCK FORM, IT COULD DROWN!
STONE HAS NO NEED TO BREATHE, ZANE. HE WILL BE SAFE ENOUGH... BUT WILL WE?

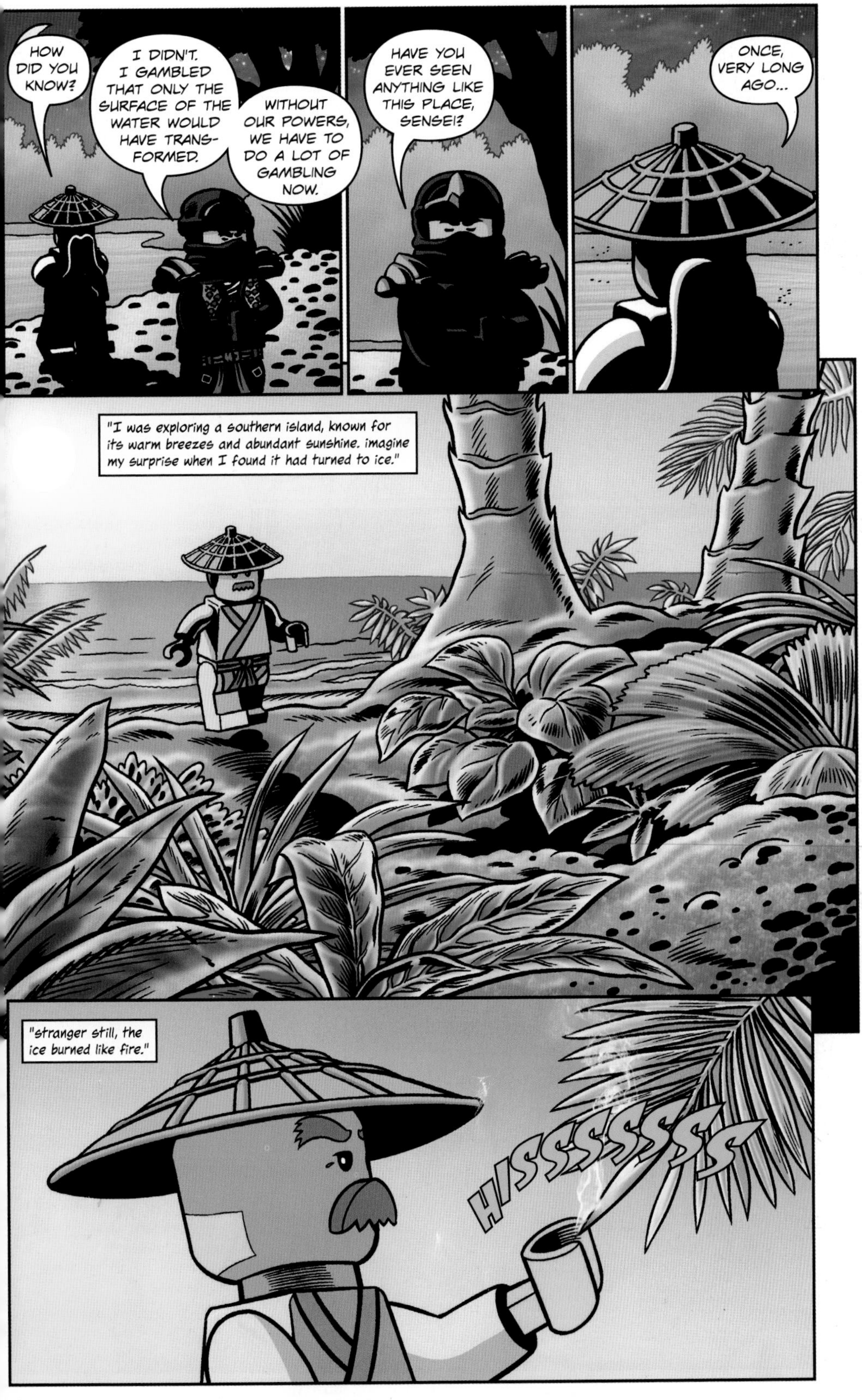
HOW DID YOU KNOW?
I DIDN'T. I GAMBLED THAT ONLY THE SURFACE OF THE WATER WOULD HAVE TRANS-FORMED.
WITHOUT OUR POWERS, WE HAVE TO DO A LOT OF GAMBLING NOW.
HAVE YOU EVER SEEN ANYTHING LIKE THIS PLACE, SENSEI?
ONCE, VERY LONG AGO...
"I was exploring a southern island, known for its warm breezes and abundant sunshine. imagine my surprise when I found it had turned to ice."
"stranger still, the ice burned like fire."
HISSSSSSS

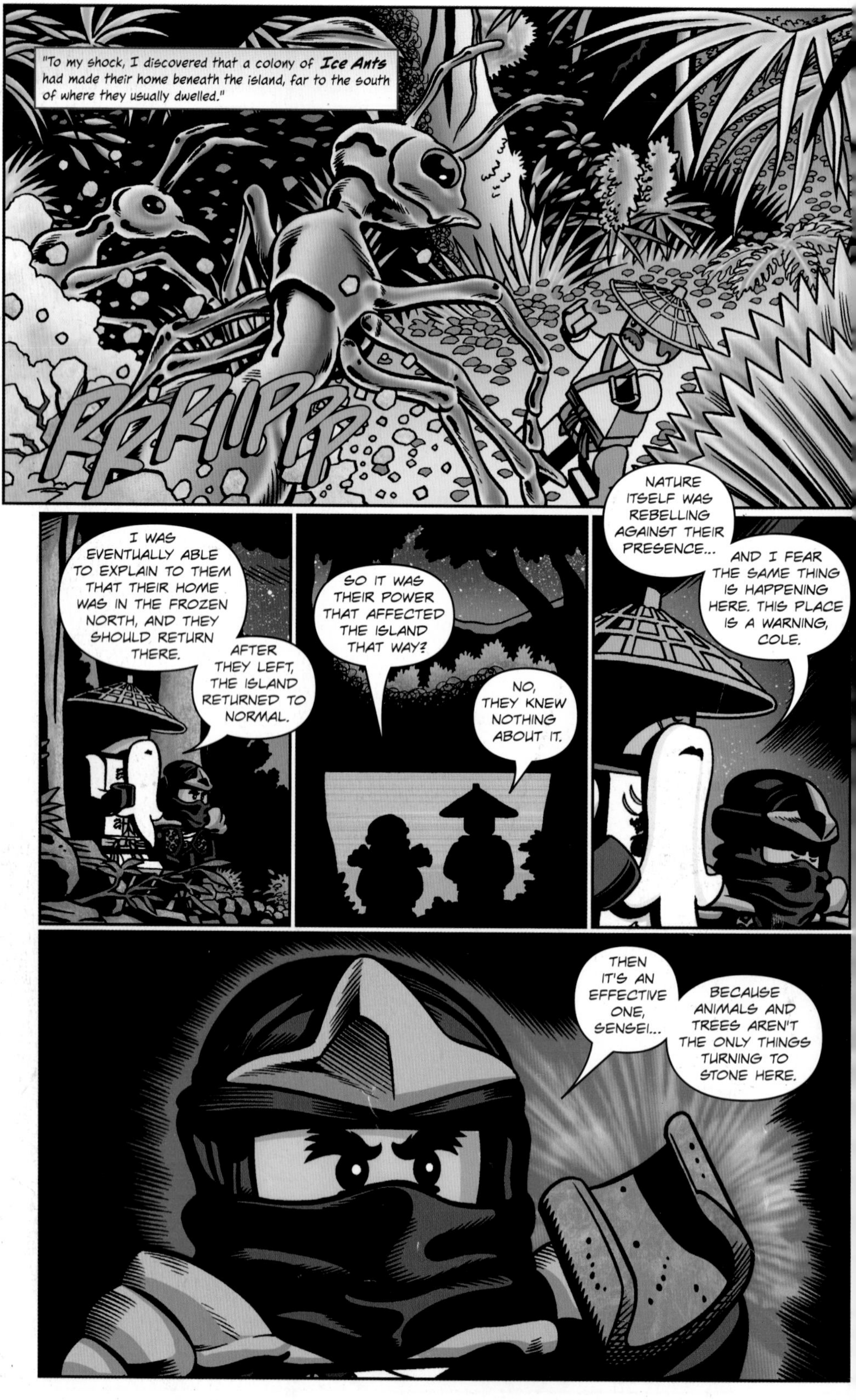
"To my shock, I discovered that a colony of Ice Ants had made their home beneath the island, far to the south of where they usually dwelled."
RRRIIPPP
I WAS EVENTUALLY ABLE TO EXPLAIN TO THEM THAT THEIR HOME WAS IN THE FROZEN NORTH, AND THEY SHOULD RETURN THERE.
AFTER THEY LEFT, THE ISLAND RETURNED TO NORMAL.
SO IT WAS THEIR POWER THAT AFFECTED THE ISLAND THAT WAY?
NO, THEY KNEW NOTHING ABOUT IT.
NATURE ITSELF WAS REBELLING AGAINST THEIR PRESENCE...
AND I FEAR THE SAME THING IS HAPPENING HERE. THIS PLACE IS A WARNING, COLE.
THEN IT'S AN EFFECTIVE ONE, SENSEI...
BECAUSE ANIMALS AND TREES AREN'T THE ONLY THINGS TURNING TO STONE HERE.

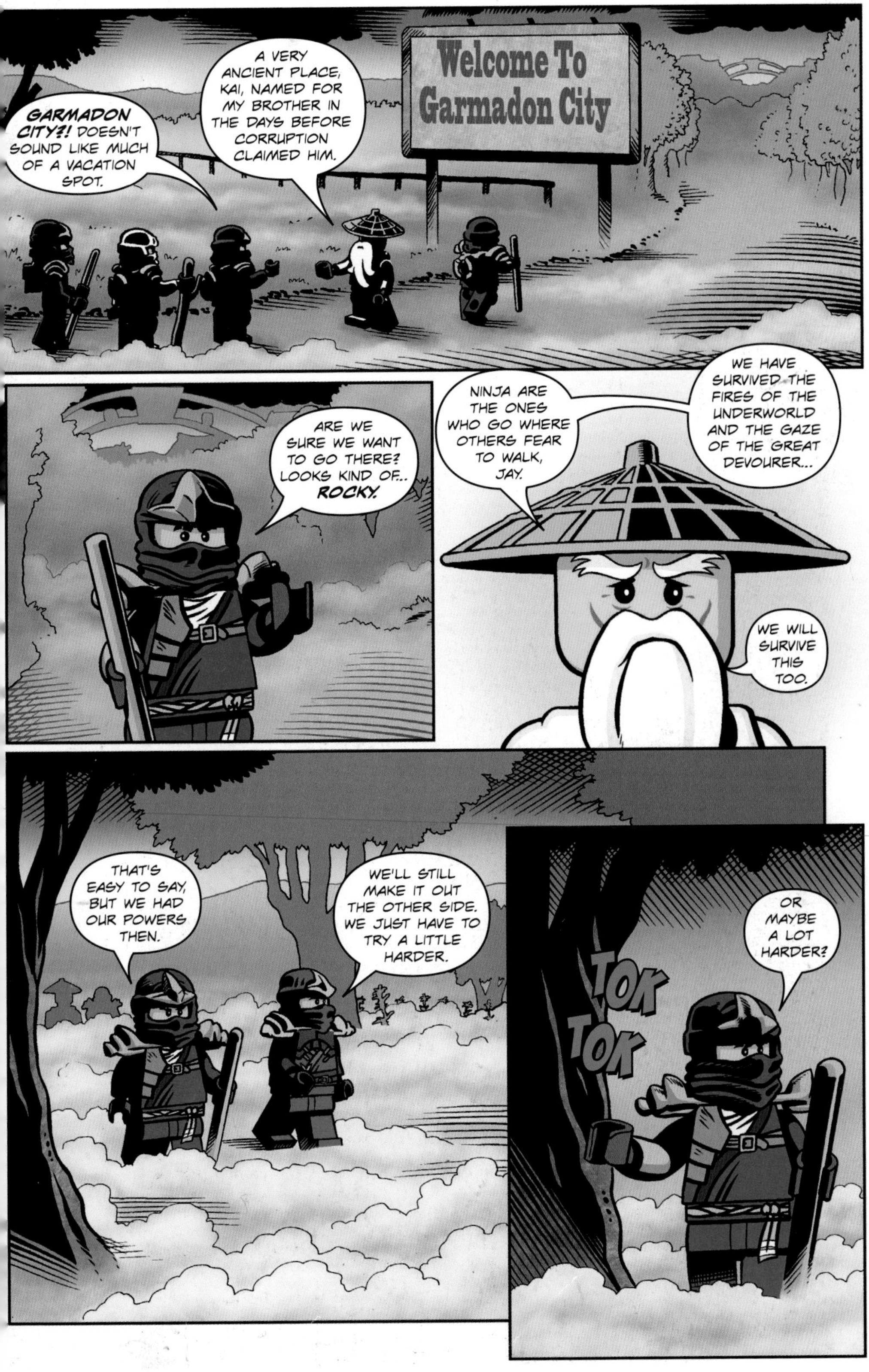
Welcome To Garmadon City
GARMADON CITY?! DOESN'T SOUND LIKE MUCH OF A VACATION SPOT.
A VERY ANCIENT PLACE, KAI, NAMED FOR MY BROTHER IN THE DAYS BEFORE CORRUPTION CLAIMED HIM.
ARE WE SURE WE WANT TO GO THERE? LOOKS KIND OF... ROCKY.
NINJA ARE THE ONES WHO GO WHERE OTHERS FEAR TO WALK, JAY.
WE HAVE SURVIVED THE FIRES OF THE UNDERWORLD AND THE GAZE OF THE GREAT DEVOURER...
WE WILL SURVIVE THIS TOO.
THAT'S EASY TO SAY, BUT WE HAD OUR POWERS THEN.
WE'LL STILL MAKE IT OUT THE OTHER SIDE. WE JUST HAVE TO TRY A LITTLE HARDER.
TOK TOK
OR MAYBE A LOT HARDER?

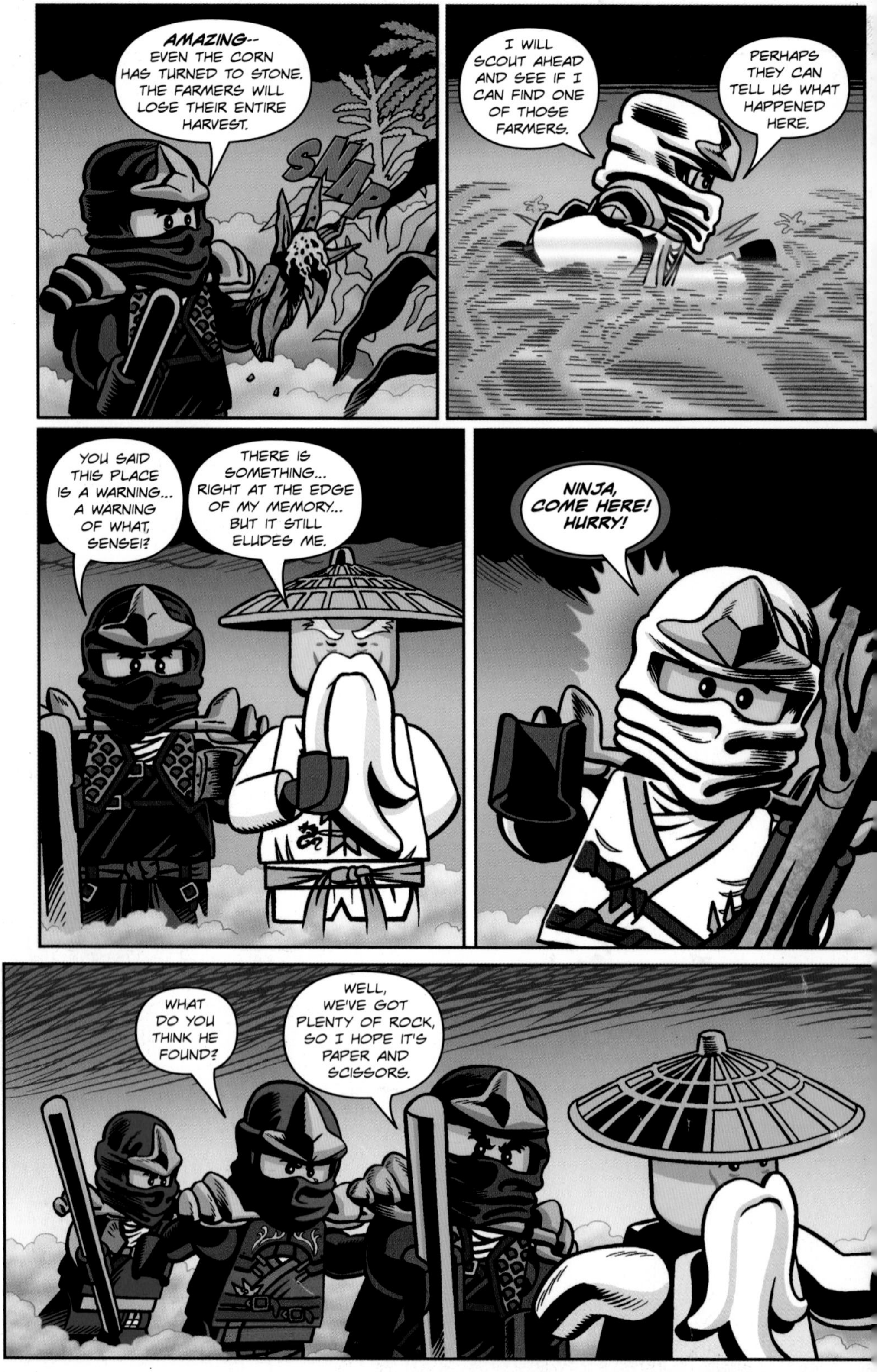
AMAZING-- EVEN THE CORN HAS TURNED TO STONE. THE FARMERS WILL LOSE THEIR ENTIRE HARVEST.
SNAP
I WILL SCOUT AHEAD AND SEE IF I CAN FIND ONE OF THOSE FARMERS.
PERHAPS THEY CAN TELL US WHAT HAPPENED HERE.
YOU SAID THIS PLACE IS A WARNING... A WARNING OF WHAT, SENSEI?
THERE IS SOMETHING... RIGHT AT THE EDGE OF MY MEMORY... BUT IT STILL ELUDES ME.
NINJA, COME HERE! HURRY!
WHAT DO YOU THINK HE FOUND?
WELL, WE'VE GOT PLENTY OF ROCK, SO I HOPE IT'S PAPER AND SCISSORS.

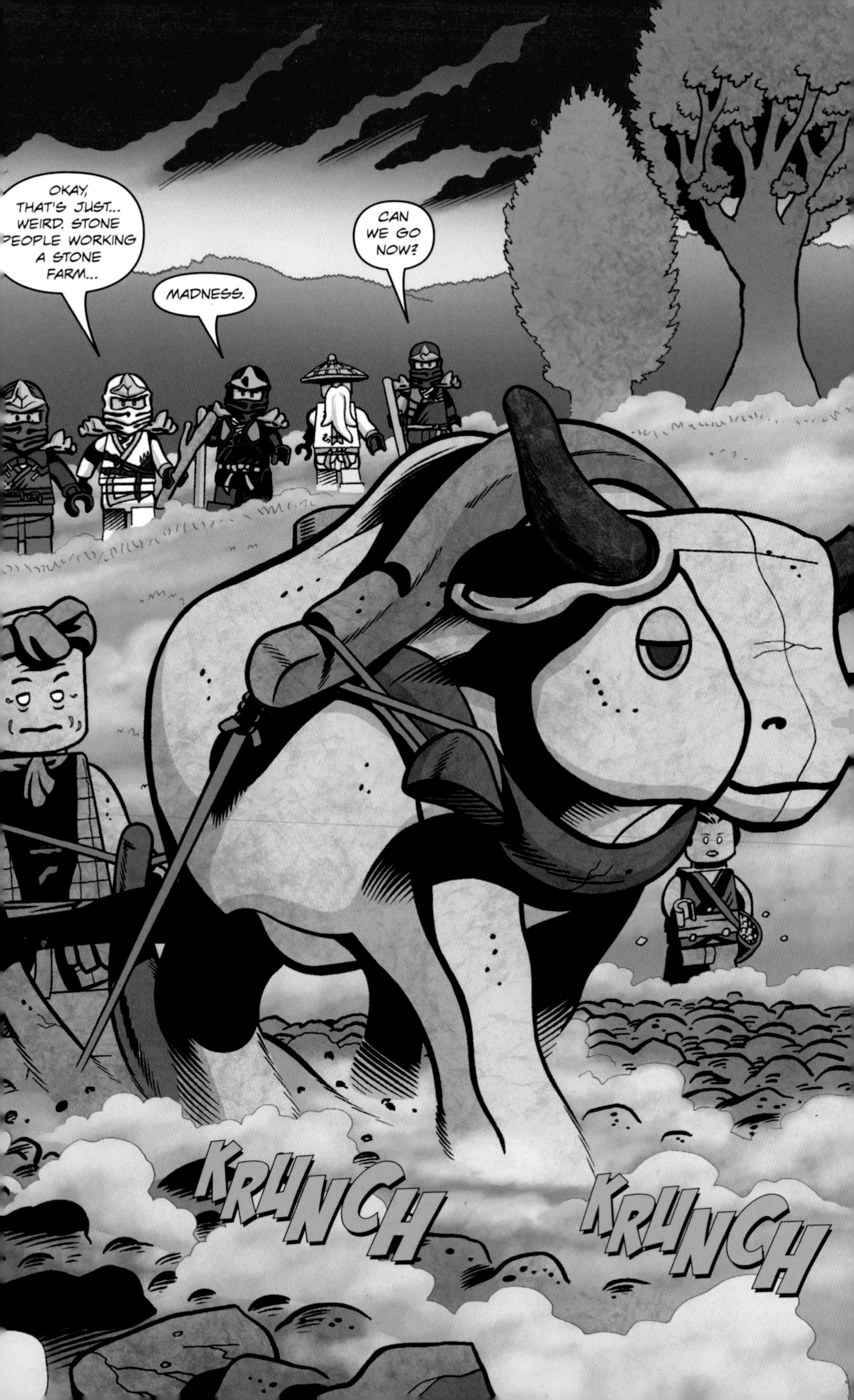
OKAY, THAT'S JUST... WEIRD. STONE PEOPLE WORKING A STONE FARM...
MADNESS.
CAN WE GO NOW?
KRUNCH
KRUNCH

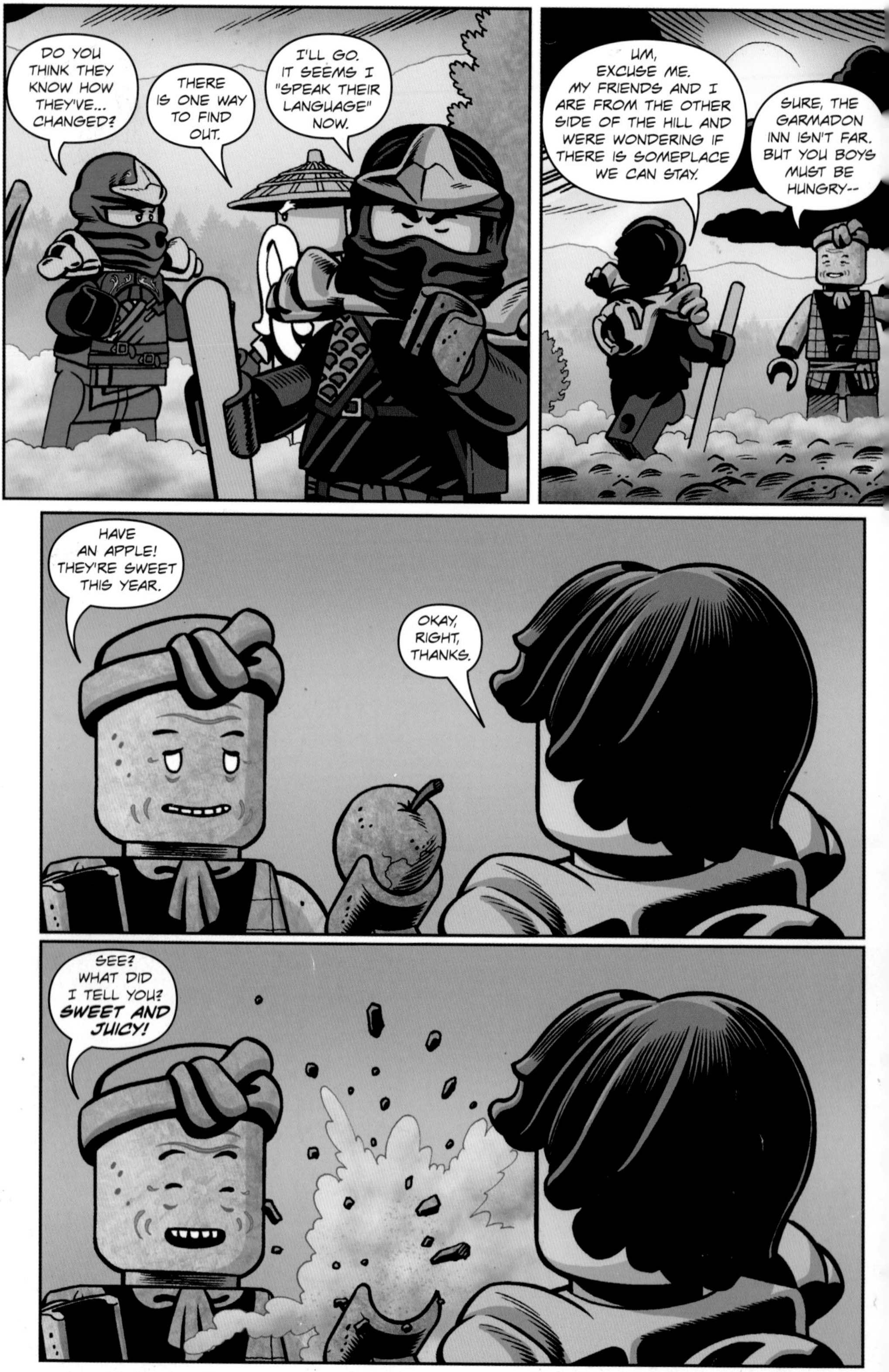
DO YOU THINK THEY KNOW HOW THEY'VE... CHANGED?
THERE IS ONE WAY TO FIND OUT.
I'LL GO. IT SEEMS I "SPEAK THEIR LANGUAGE" NOW.
UM, EXCUSE ME. MY FRIENDS AND I ARE FROM THE OTHER SIDE OF THE HILL AND WERE WONDERING IF THERE IS SOMEPLACE WE CAN STAY.
SURE, THE GARMADON INN ISN'T FAR. BUT YOU BOYS MUST BE HUNGRY--
HAVE AN APPLE! THEY'RE SWEET THIS YEAR.
OKAY, RIGHT, THANKS.
SEE? WHAT DID I TELL YOU? ***SWEET AND JUICY!***

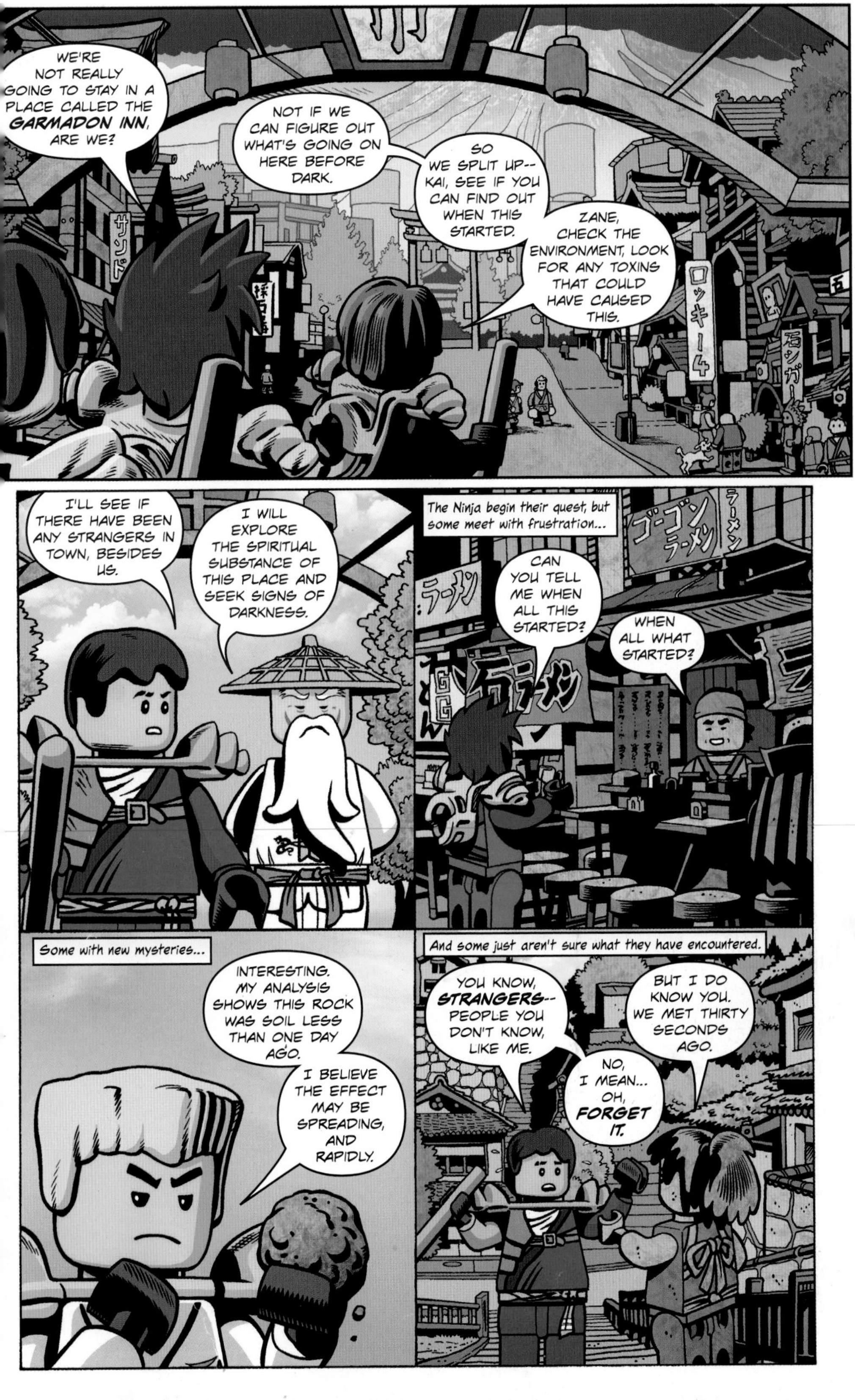

WE'RE NOT REALLY GOING TO STAY IN A PLACE CALLED THE GARMADON INN, ARE WE?
NOT IF WE CAN FIGURE OUT WHAT'S GOING ON HERE BEFORE DARK.
SO WE SPLIT UP-- KAI, SEE IF YOU CAN FIND OUT WHEN THIS STARTED.
ZANE, CHECK THE ENVIRONMENT, LOOK FOR ANY TOXINS THAT COULD HAVE CAUSED THIS.
I'LL SEE IF THERE HAVE BEEN ANY STRANGERS IN TOWN, BESIDES US.
I WILL EXPLORE THE SPIRITUAL SUBSTANCE OF THIS PLACE AND SEEK SIGNS OF DARKNESS.
The Ninja begin their quest, but some meet with frustration...
CAN YOU TELL ME WHEN ALL THIS STARTED?
WHEN ALL WHAT STARTED?
Some with new mysteries...
INTERESTING. MY ANALYSIS SHOWS THIS ROCK WAS SOIL LESS THAN ONE DAY AGO.
I BELIEVE THE EFFECT MAY BE SPREADING, AND RAPIDLY.
And some just aren't sure what they have encountered.
YOU KNOW, STRANGERS-- PEOPLE YOU DON'T KNOW, LIKE ME.
BUT I DO KNOW YOU. WE MET THIRTY SECONDS AGO.
NO, I MEAN... OH, FORGET IT.

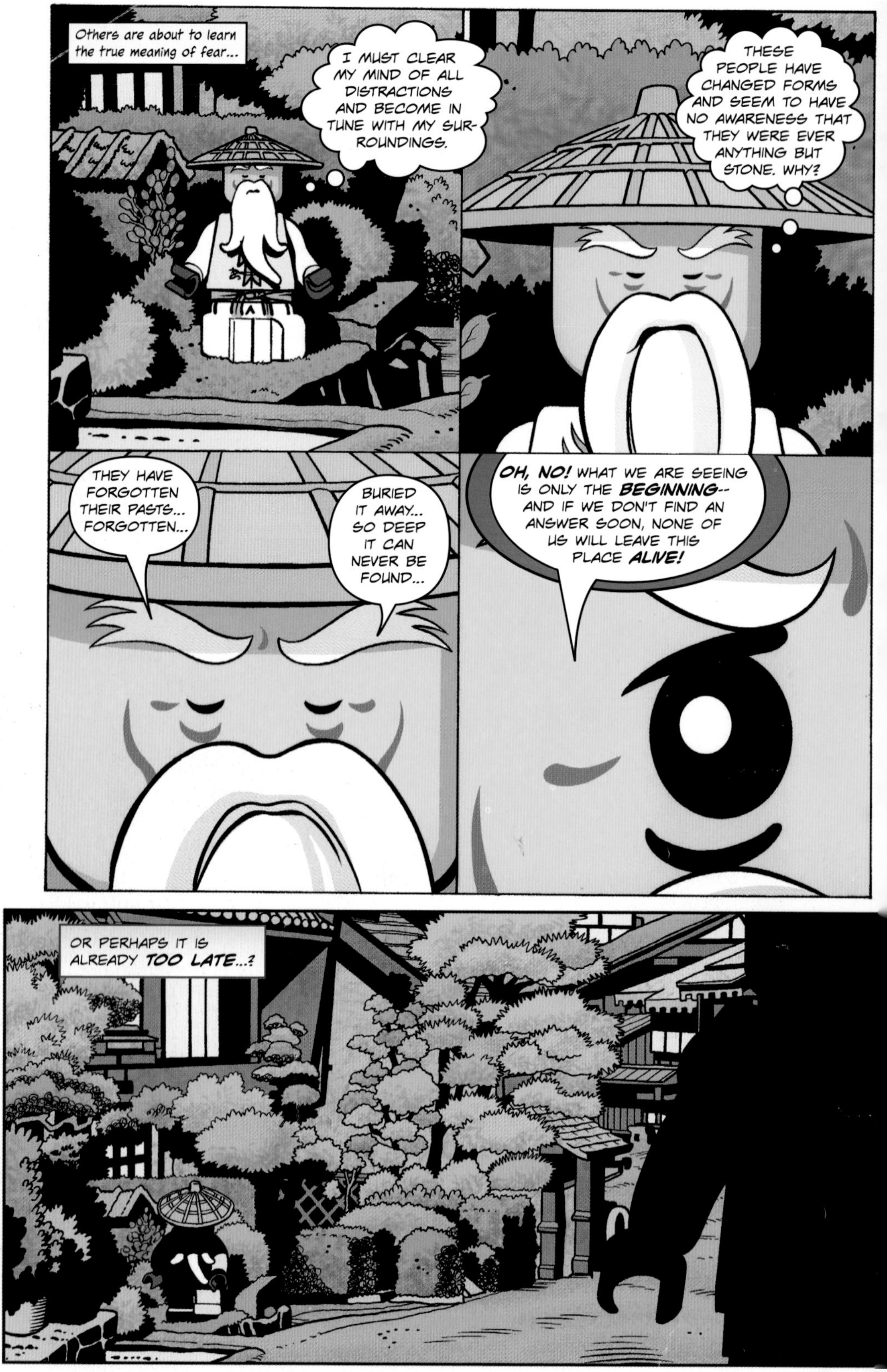
Others are about to learn the true meaning of fear...
I MUST CLEAR MY MIND OF ALL DISTRACTIONS AND BECOME IN TUNE WITH MY SURROUNDINGS.
THESE PEOPLE HAVE CHANGED FORMS AND SEEM TO HAVE NO AWARENESS THAT THEY WERE EVER ANYTHING BUT STONE. WHY?
THEY HAVE FORGOTTEN THEIR PASTS... FORGOTTEN...
BURIED IT AWAY... SO DEEP IT CAN NEVER BE FOUND...
OH, NO! WHAT WE ARE SEEING IS ONLY THE BEGINNING-- AND IF WE DON'T FIND AN ANSWER SOON, NONE OF US WILL LEAVE THIS PLACE ALIVE!
OR PERHAPS IT IS ALREADY TOO LATE...?

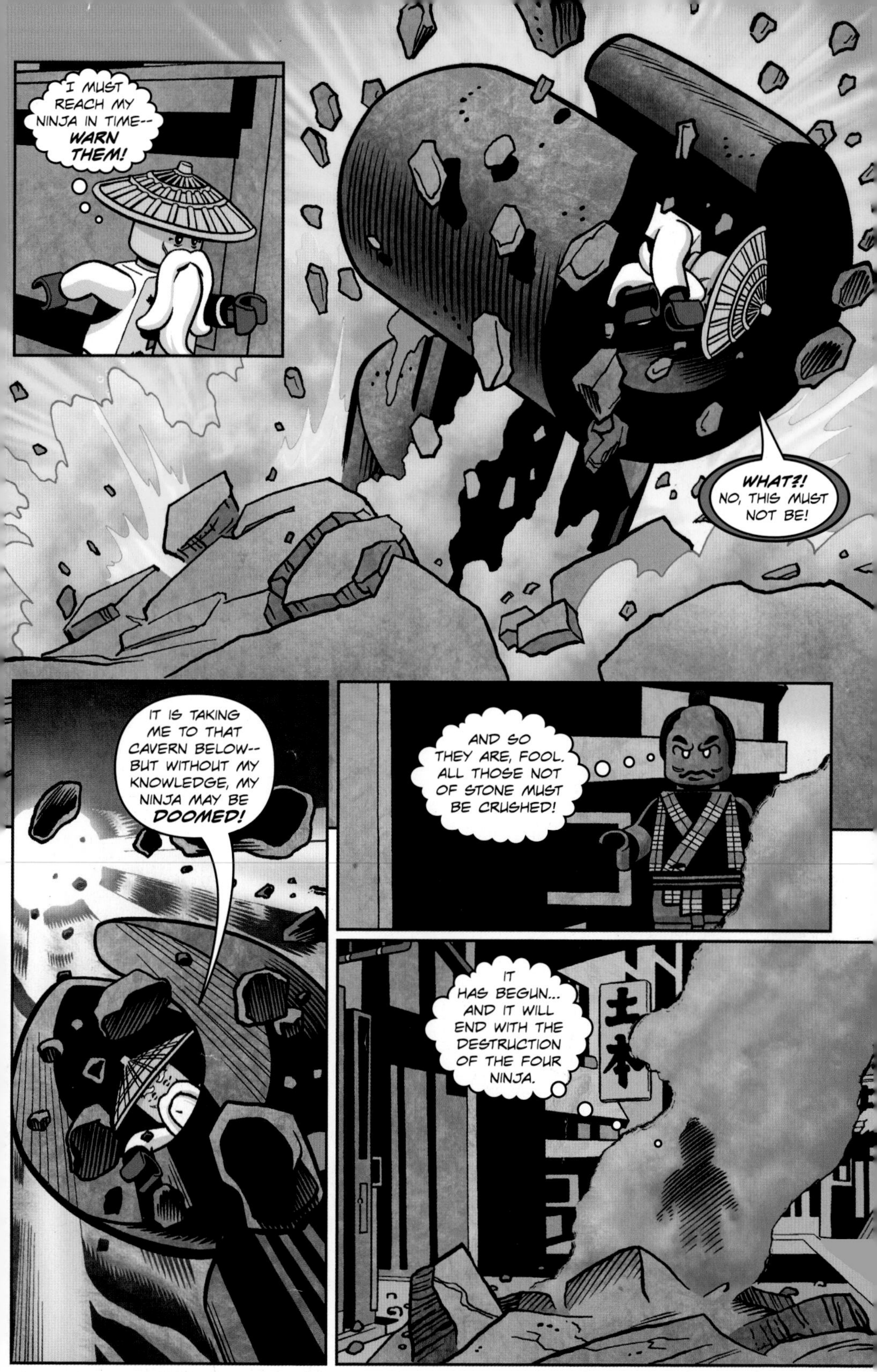
I MUST REACH MY NINJA IN TIME-- WARN THEM!
WHAT?! NO, THIS MUST NOT BE!
IT IS TAKING ME TO THAT CAVERN BELOW-- BUT WITHOUT MY KNOWLEDGE, MY NINJA MAY BE DOOMED!
AND SO THEY ARE, FOOL. ALL THOSE NOT OF STONE MUST BE CRUSHED!
IT HAS BEGUN... AND IT WILL END WITH THE DESTRUCTION OF THE FOUR NINJA.

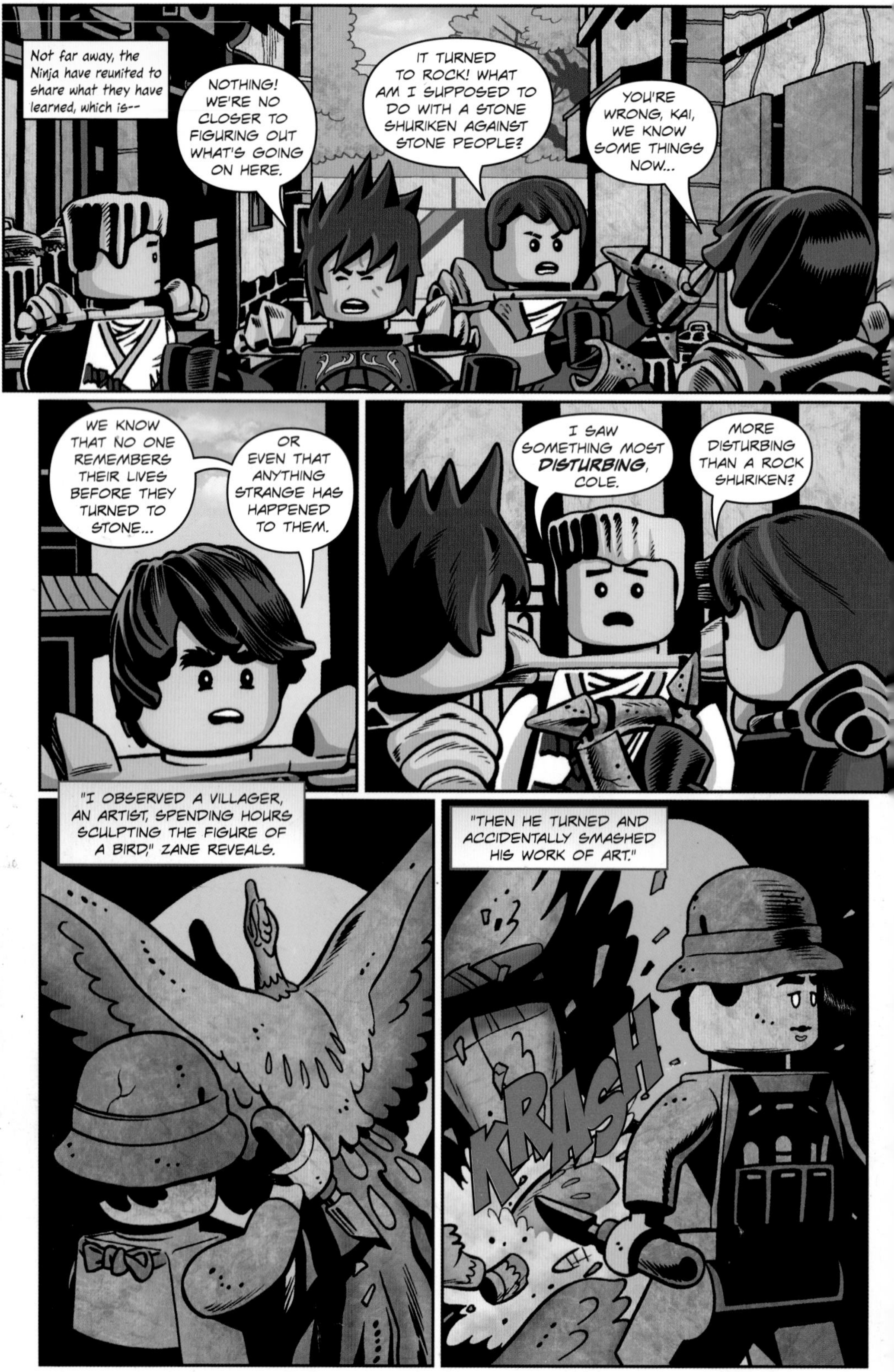

Not far away, the Ninja have reunited to share what they have learned, which is--
NOTHING! WE'RE NO CLOSER TO FIGURING OUT WHAT'S GOING ON HERE.
IT TURNED TO ROCK! WHAT AM I SUPPOSED TO DO WITH A STONE SHURIKEN AGAINST STONE PEOPLE?
YOU'RE WRONG, KAI, WE KNOW SOME THINGS NOW...
WE KNOW THAT NO ONE REMEMBERS THEIR LIVES BEFORE THEY TURNED TO STONE...
OR EVEN THAT ANYTHING STRANGE HAS HAPPENED TO THEM.
I SAW SOMETHING MOST DISTURBING, COLE.
MORE DISTURBING THAN A ROCK SHURIKEN?
"I OBSERVED A VILLAGER, AN ARTIST, SPENDING HOURS SCULPTING THE FIGURE OF A BIRD," ZANE REVEALS.
"THEN HE TURNED AND ACCIDENTALLY SMASHED HIS WORK OF ART."
KRASH

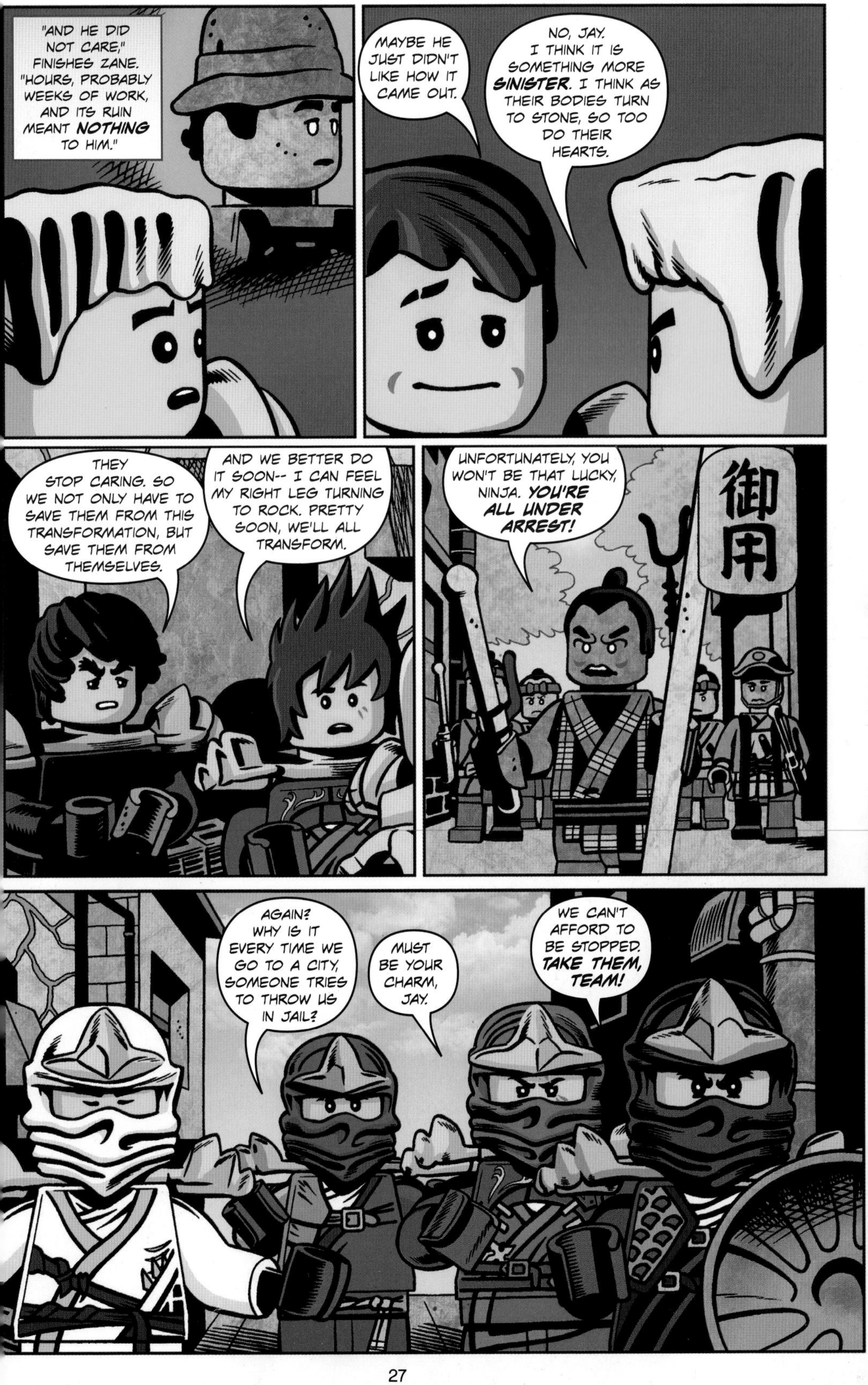
"AND HE DID NOT CARE," FINISHES ZANE. "HOURS, PROBABLY WEEKS OF WORK, AND ITS RUIN MEANT **NOTHING** TO HIM."
MAYBE HE JUST DIDN'T LIKE HOW IT CAME OUT.
NO, JAY. I THINK IT IS SOMETHING MORE **SINISTER**. I THINK AS THEIR BODIES TURN TO STONE, SO TOO DO THEIR HEARTS.
THEY STOP CARING. SO WE NOT ONLY HAVE TO SAVE THEM FROM THIS TRANSFORMATION, BUT SAVE THEM FROM THEMSELVES.
AND WE BETTER DO IT SOON-- I CAN FEEL MY RIGHT LEG TURNING TO ROCK. PRETTY SOON, WE'LL ALL TRANSFORM.
UNFORTUNATELY, YOU WON'T BE THAT LUCKY, NINJA. **YOU'RE ALL UNDER ARREST!**
御用
AGAIN? WHY IS IT EVERY TIME WE GO TO A CITY, SOMEONE TRIES TO THROW US IN JAIL?
MUST BE YOUR CHARM, JAY.
WE CAN'T AFFORD TO BE STOPPED. **TAKE THEM, TEAM!**

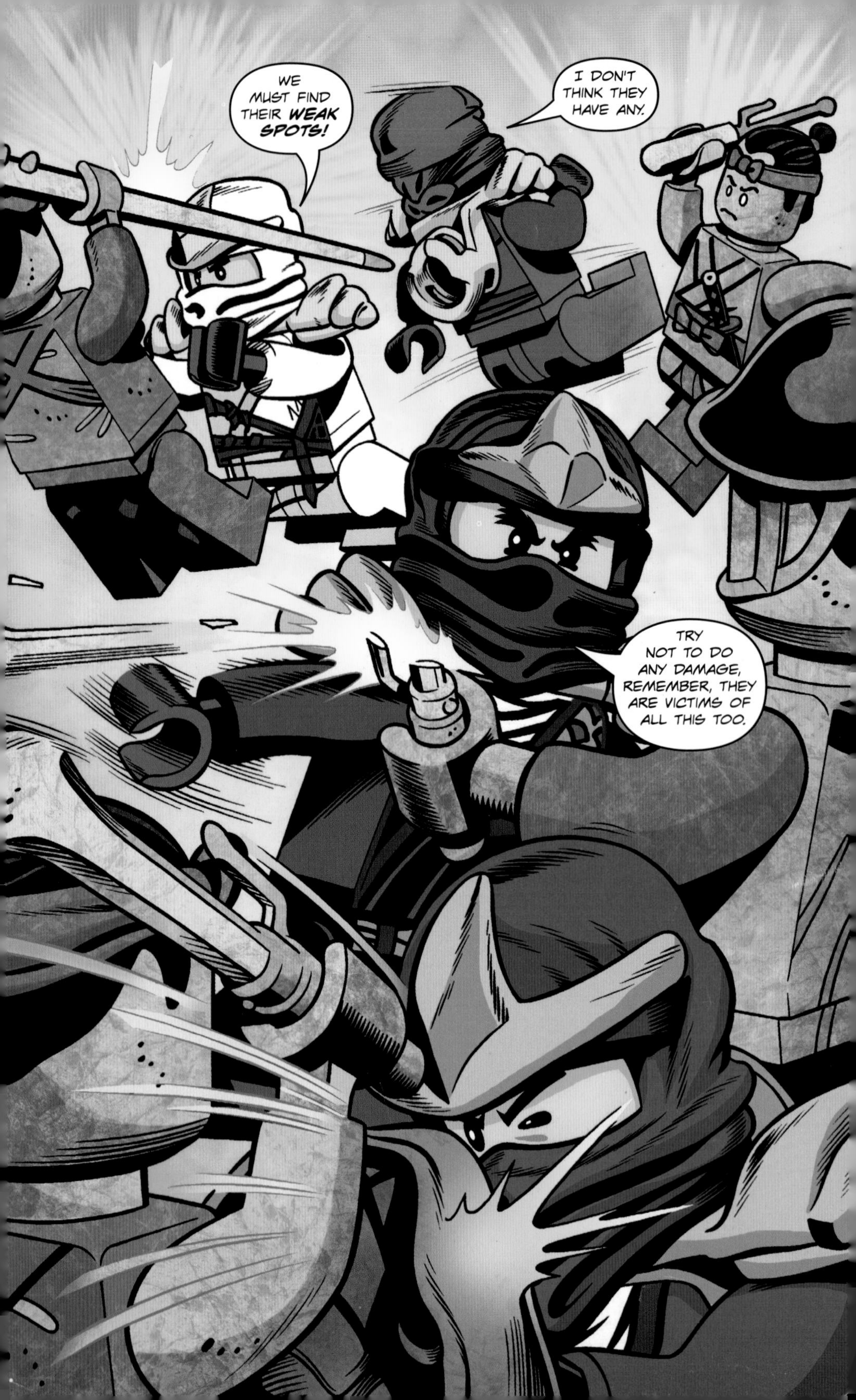

WE MUST FIND THEIR **WEAK SPOTS!**
I DON'T THINK THEY HAVE ANY.
TRY NOT TO DO ANY DAMAGE, REMEMBER, THEY ARE VICTIMS OF ALL THIS TOO.

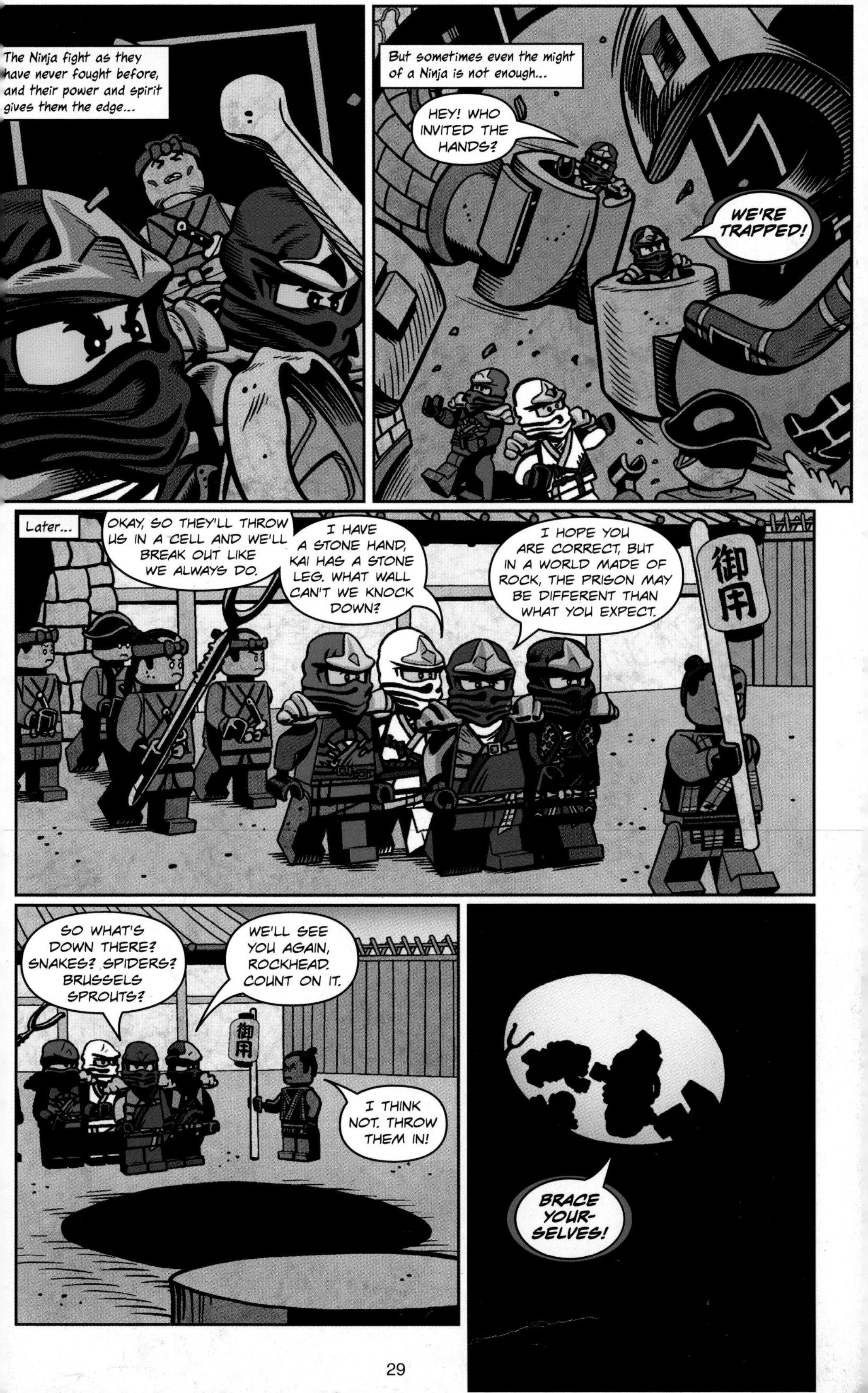

The Ninja fight as they have never fought before, and their power and spirit gives them the edge...
But sometimes even the might of a Ninja is not enough...
HEY! WHO INVITED THE HANDS?
WE'RE TRAPPED!
Later...
OKAY, SO THEY'LL THROW US IN A CELL AND WE'LL BREAK OUT LIKE WE ALWAYS DO.
I HAVE A STONE HAND, KAI HAS A STONE LEG. WHAT WALL CAN'T WE KNOCK DOWN?
I HOPE YOU ARE CORRECT, BUT IN A WORLD MADE OF ROCK, THE PRISON MAY BE DIFFERENT THAN WHAT YOU EXPECT.
御用
SO WHAT'S DOWN THERE? SNAKES? SPIDERS? BRUSSELS SPROUTS?
WE'LL SEE YOU AGAIN, ROCKHEAD. COUNT ON IT.
御用
I THINK NOT. THROW THEM IN!
BRACE YOUR-SELVES!

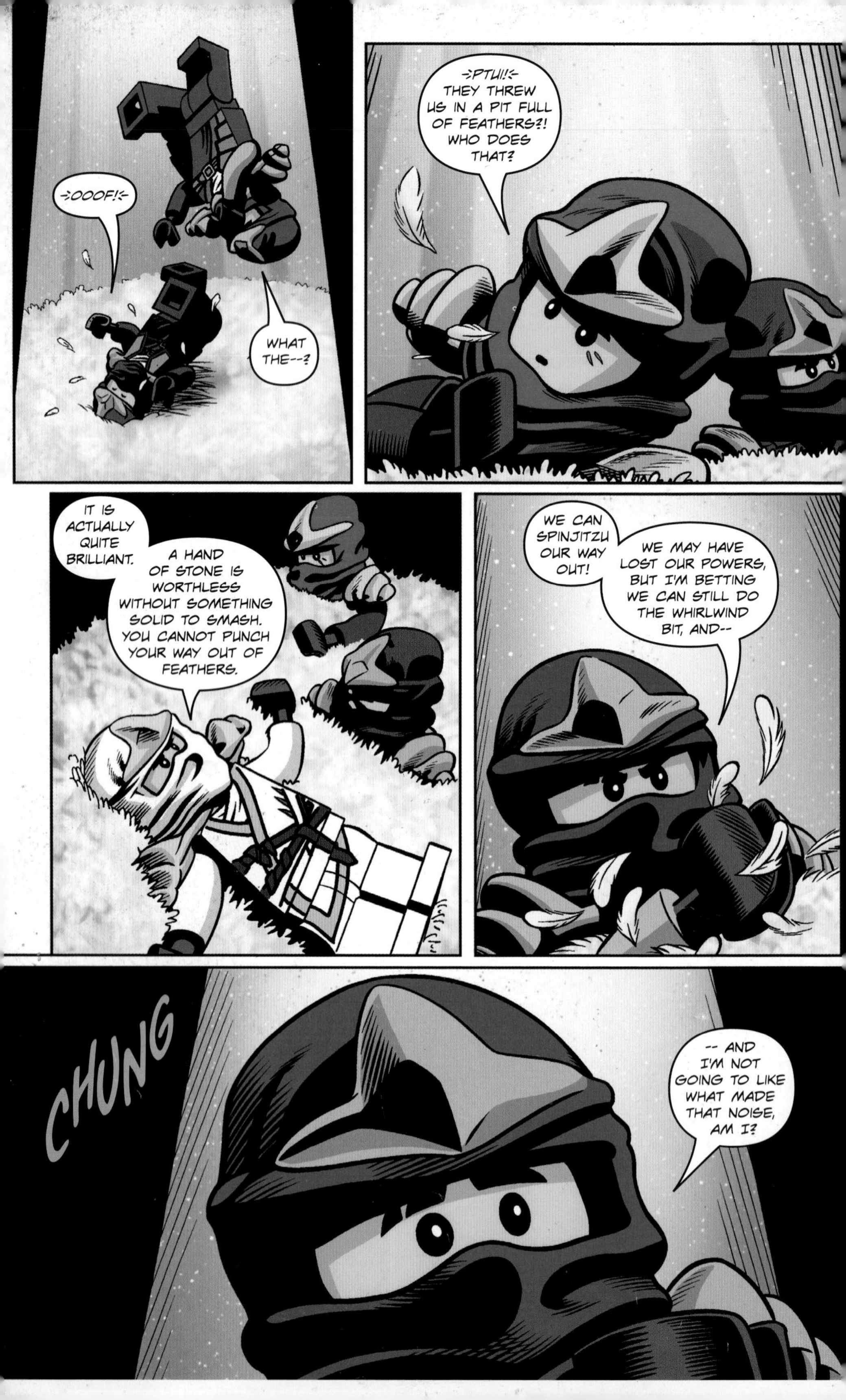

>OOOF!<
WHAT THE--?
>PTUI!< THEY THREW US IN A PIT FULL OF FEATHERS?! WHO DOES THAT?
IT IS ACTUALLY QUITE BRILLIANT.
A HAND OF STONE IS WORTHLESS WITHOUT SOMETHING SOLID TO SMASH. YOU CANNOT PUNCH YOUR WAY OUT OF FEATHERS.
WE CAN SPINJITZU OUR WAY OUT!
WE MAY HAVE LOST OUR POWERS, BUT I'M BETTING WE CAN STILL DO THE WHIRLWIND BIT, AND--
CHUNG
-- AND I'M NOT GOING TO LIKE WHAT MADE THAT NOISE, AM I?

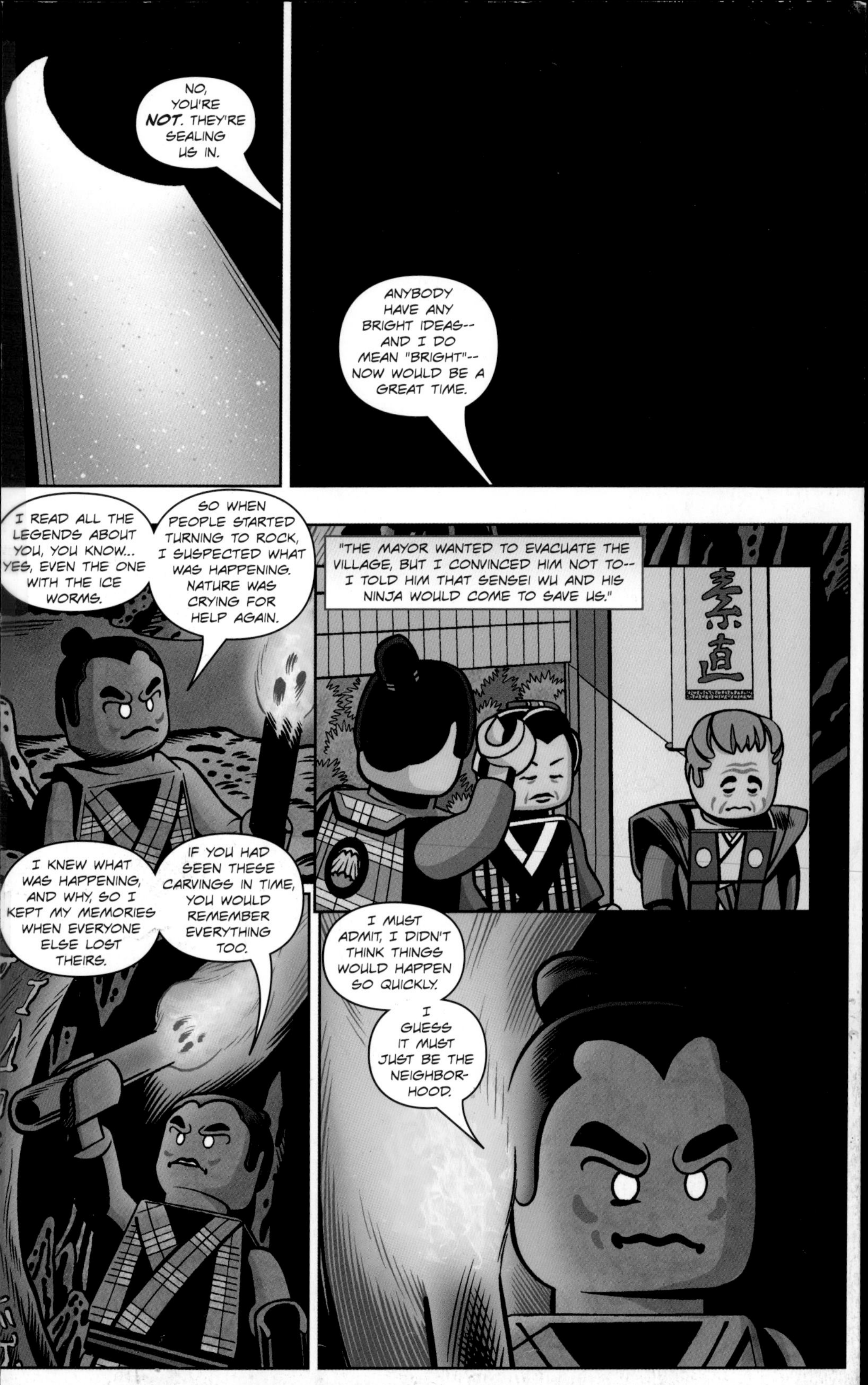
NO, YOU'RE *NOT*. THEY'RE SEALING US IN.
ANYBODY HAVE ANY BRIGHT IDEAS-- AND I DO MEAN "BRIGHT"-- NOW WOULD BE A GREAT TIME.
I READ ALL THE LEGENDS ABOUT YOU, YOU KNOW... YES, EVEN THE ONE WITH THE ICE WORMS.
SO WHEN PEOPLE STARTED TURNING TO ROCK, I SUSPECTED WHAT WAS HAPPENING. NATURE WAS CRYING FOR HELP AGAIN.
"THE MAYOR WANTED TO EVACUATE THE VILLAGE, BUT I CONVINCED HIM NOT TO-- I TOLD HIM THAT SENSEI WU AND HIS NINJA WOULD COME TO SAVE US."
I KNEW WHAT WAS HAPPENING, AND WHY, SO I KEPT MY MEMORIES WHEN EVERYONE ELSE LOST THEIRS.
IF YOU HAD SEEN THESE CARVINGS IN TIME, YOU WOULD REMEMBER EVERYTHING TOO.
I MUST ADMIT, I DIDN'T THINK THINGS WOULD HAPPEN SO QUICKLY.
I GUESS IT MUST JUST BE THE NEIGHBOR-HOOD.

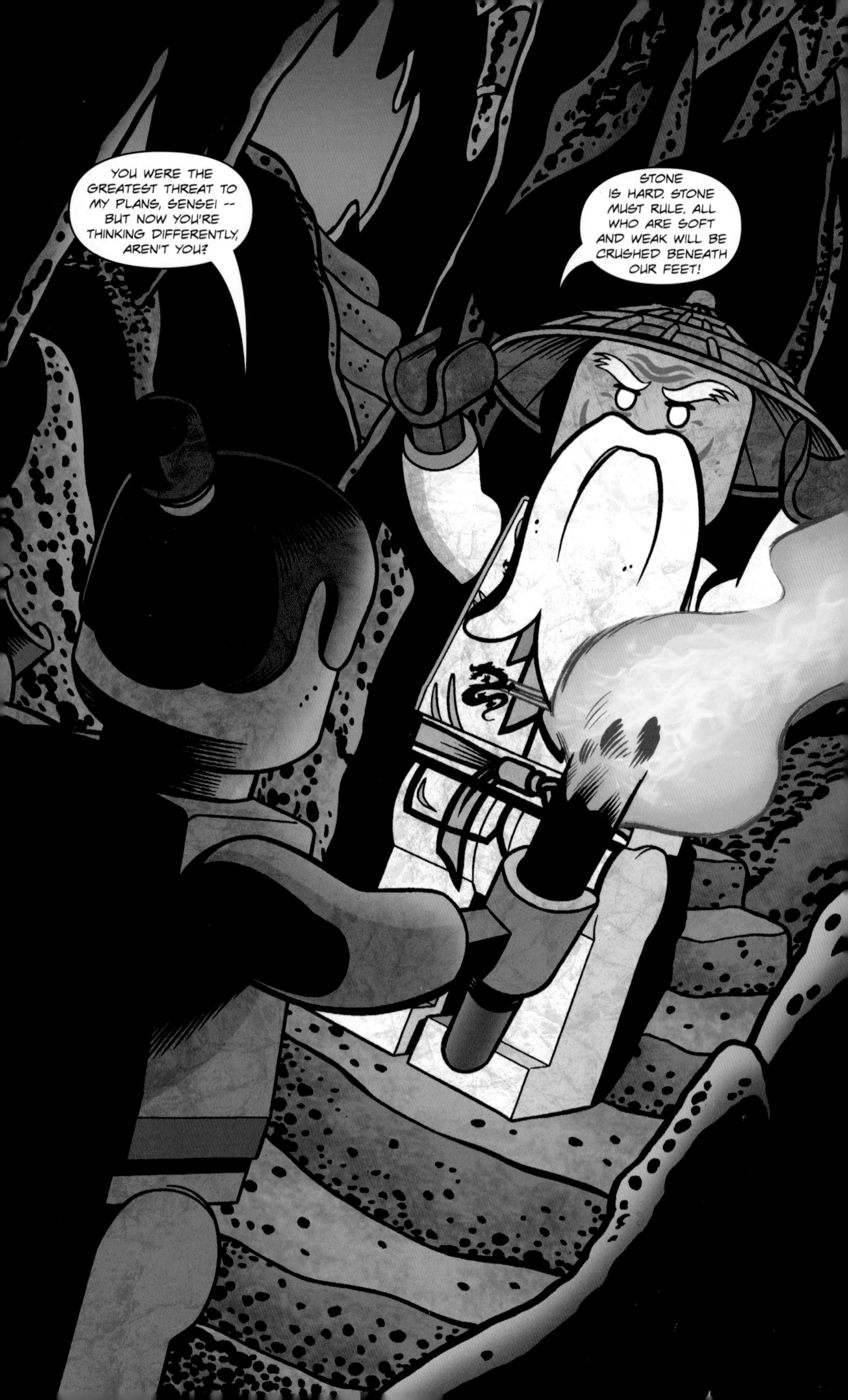
YOU WERE THE GREATEST THREAT TO MY PLANS, SENSEI -- BUT NOW YOU'RE THINKING DIFFERENTLY, AREN'T YOU?
STONE IS HARD. STONE MUST RULE. ALL WHO ARE SOFT AND WEAK WILL BE CRUSHED BENEATH OUR FEET!

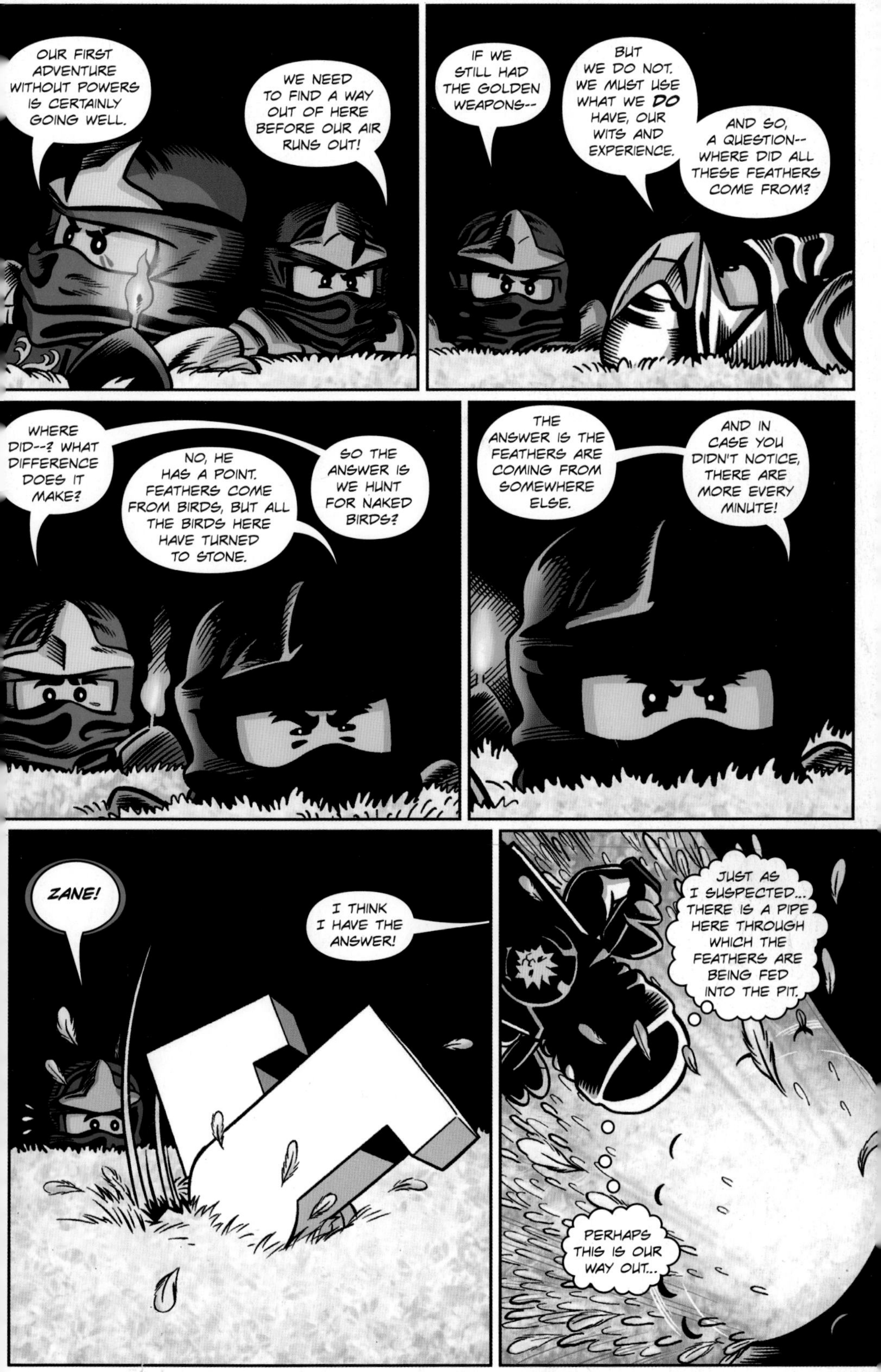

OUR FIRST ADVENTURE WITHOUT POWERS IS CERTAINLY GOING WELL.
WE NEED TO FIND A WAY OUT OF HERE BEFORE OUR AIR RUNS OUT!
IF WE STILL HAD THE GOLDEN WEAPONS--
BUT WE DO NOT. WE MUST USE WHAT WE **DO** HAVE, OUR WITS AND EXPERIENCE.
AND SO, A QUESTION-- WHERE DID ALL THESE FEATHERS COME FROM?
WHERE DID--? WHAT DIFFERENCE DOES IT MAKE?
NO, HE HAS A POINT. FEATHERS COME FROM BIRDS, BUT ALL THE BIRDS HERE HAVE TURNED TO STONE.
SO THE ANSWER IS WE HUNT FOR NAKED BIRDS?
THE ANSWER IS THE FEATHERS ARE COMING FROM SOMEWHERE ELSE.
AND IN CASE YOU DIDN'T NOTICE, THERE ARE MORE EVERY MINUTE!
ZANE!
I THINK I HAVE THE ANSWER!
JUST AS I SUSPECTED... THERE IS A PIPE HERE THROUGH WHICH THE FEATHERS ARE BEING FED INTO THE PIT.
PERHAPS THIS IS OUR WAY OUT...

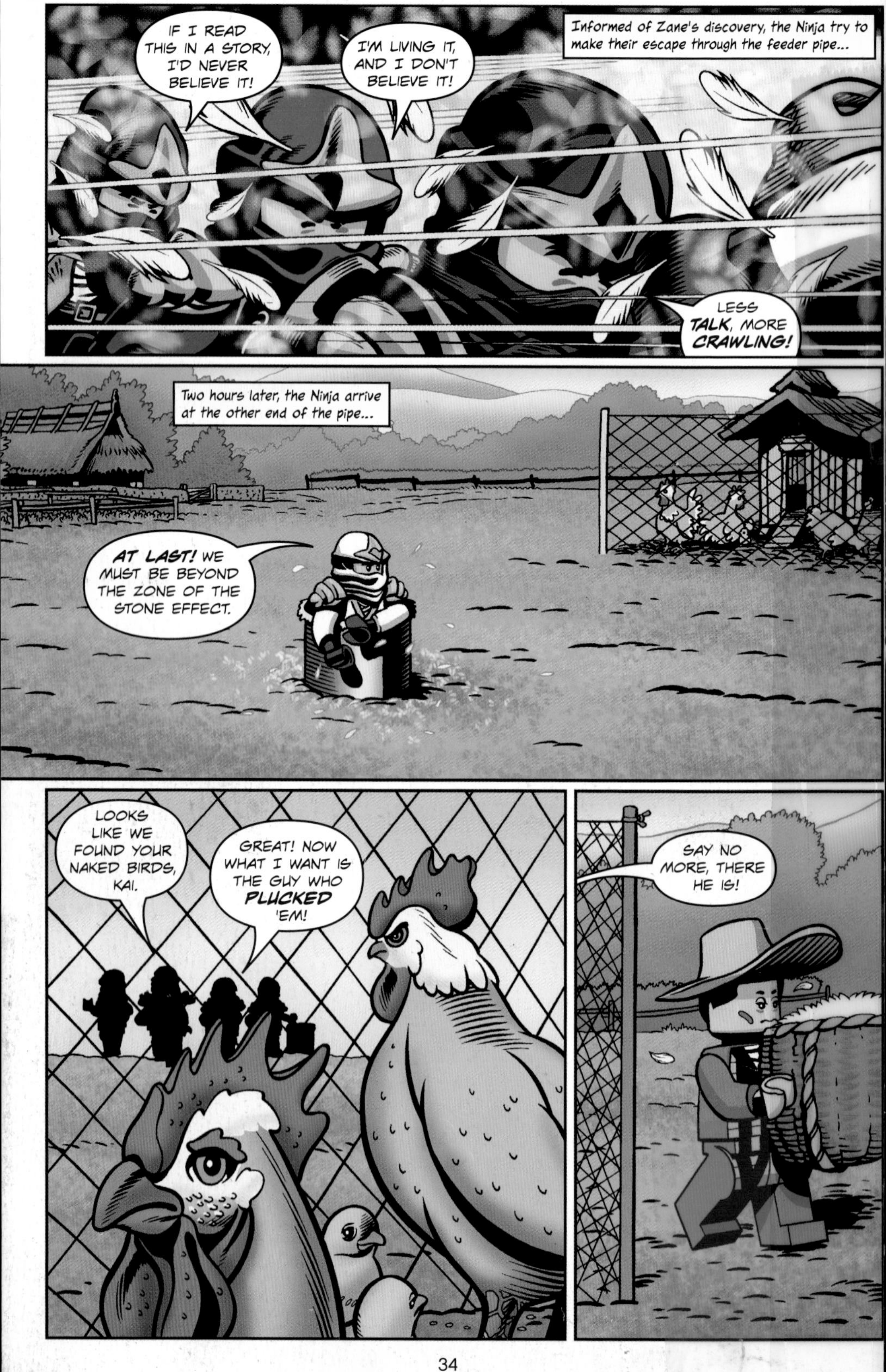
Informed of Zane's discovery, the Ninja try to make their escape through the feeder pipe...
IF I READ THIS IN A STORY, I'D NEVER BELIEVE IT!
I'M LIVING IT, AND I DON'T BELIEVE IT!
LESS TALK, MORE CRAWLING!
Two hours later, the Ninja arrive at the other end of the pipe...
AT LAST! WE MUST BE BEYOND THE ZONE OF THE STONE EFFECT.
LOOKS LIKE WE FOUND YOUR NAKED BIRDS, KAI.
GREAT! NOW WHAT I WANT IS THE GUY WHO PLUCKED 'EM!
SAY NO MORE, THERE HE IS!

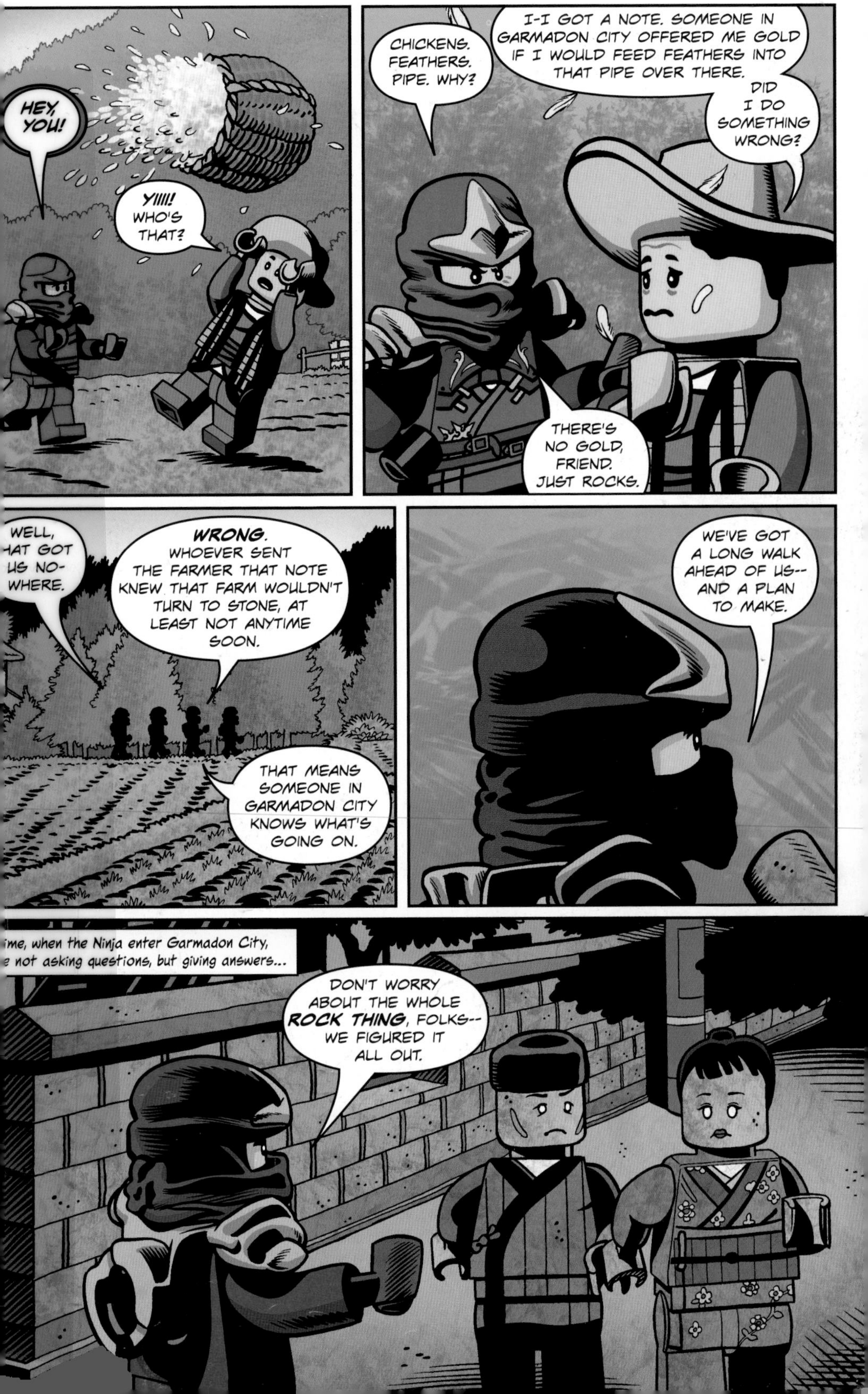
HEY, YOU!
YIIII! WHO'S THAT?
CHICKENS. FEATHERS. PIPE. WHY?
I-I GOT A NOTE. SOMEONE IN GARMADON CITY OFFERED ME GOLD IF I WOULD FEED FEATHERS INTO THAT PIPE OVER THERE.
DID I DO SOMETHING WRONG?
THERE'S NO GOLD, FRIEND. JUST ROCKS.
WELL, HAT GOT US NO-WHERE.
WRONG. WHOEVER SENT THE FARMER THAT NOTE KNEW THAT FARM WOULDN'T TURN TO STONE, AT LEAST NOT ANYTIME SOON.
THAT MEANS SOMEONE IN GARMADON CITY KNOWS WHAT'S GOING ON.
WE'VE GOT A LONG WALK AHEAD OF US-- AND A PLAN TO MAKE.
ime, when the Ninja enter Garmadon City,
e not asking questions, but giving answers...
DON'T WORRY ABOUT THE WHOLE ROCK THING, FOLKS-- WE FIGURED IT ALL OUT.

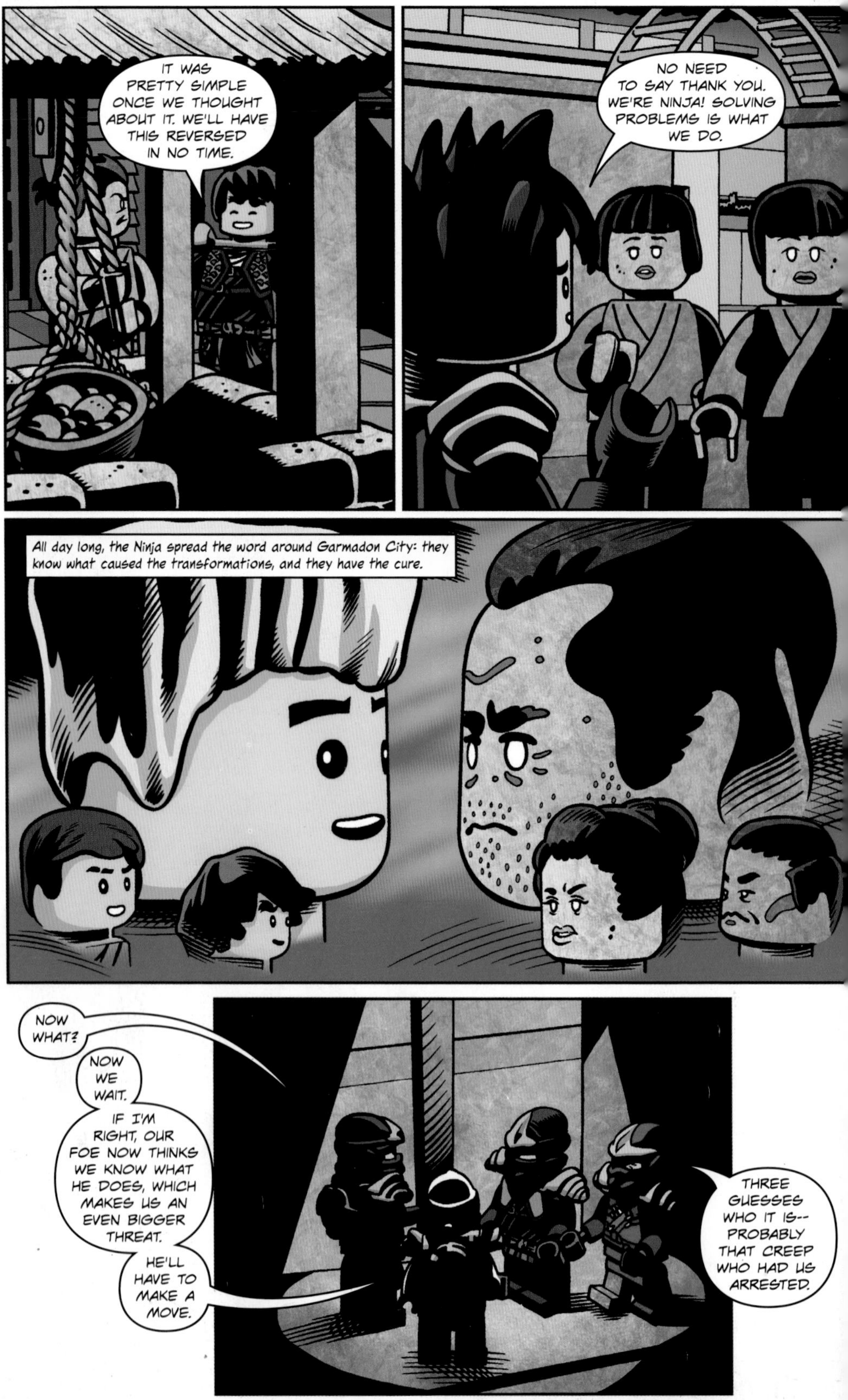
IT WAS PRETTY SIMPLE ONCE WE THOUGHT ABOUT IT. WE'LL HAVE THIS REVERSED IN NO TIME.
NO NEED TO SAY THANK YOU. WE'RE NINJA! SOLVING PROBLEMS IS WHAT WE DO.
All day long, the Ninja spread the word around Garmadon City: they know what caused the transformations, and they have the cure.
NOW WHAT?
NOW WE WAIT.
IF I'M RIGHT, OUR FOE NOW THINKS WE KNOW WHAT HE DOES, WHICH MAKES US AN EVEN BIGGER THREAT.
HE'LL HAVE TO MAKE A MOVE.
THREE GUESSES WHO IT IS-- PROBABLY THAT CREEP WHO HAD US ARRESTED.

WHOA! I'M REALLY STARTING TO HATE THIS TOWN.

"IF YOU WANT TO SAVE GARMADON CITY, MEET ME IN THE REAR OF THE SCULPTOR'S SHOP AT MIDNIGHT. SIGNED, A FRIEND."

OF COURSE, IT IS A TRAP.

NATURALLY.

WHEN HAS THAT EVER STOPPED US?

OKAY, WE'RE IN A YARD FULL OF STONE STATUES-- OR ARE THEY STATUES?

SOME OF THEM COULD BE OUR FRIENDS WITH THE CLUBS. HOW COULD WE TELL?

IF THEY TRY TO HIT YOU, THEY'RE REAL.

SPREAD OUT. LOOK AROUND.

LOOK AROUND, HE SAYS.

PITCH DARK IN A CREEPY ROCK GARDEN AND WE'RE SUPPOSED TO SIGHT-SEE.

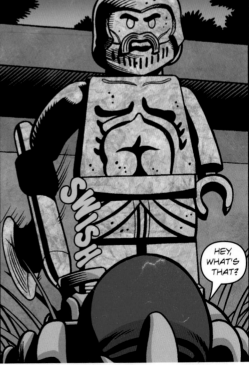

SWISH

HEY, WHAT'S THAT?

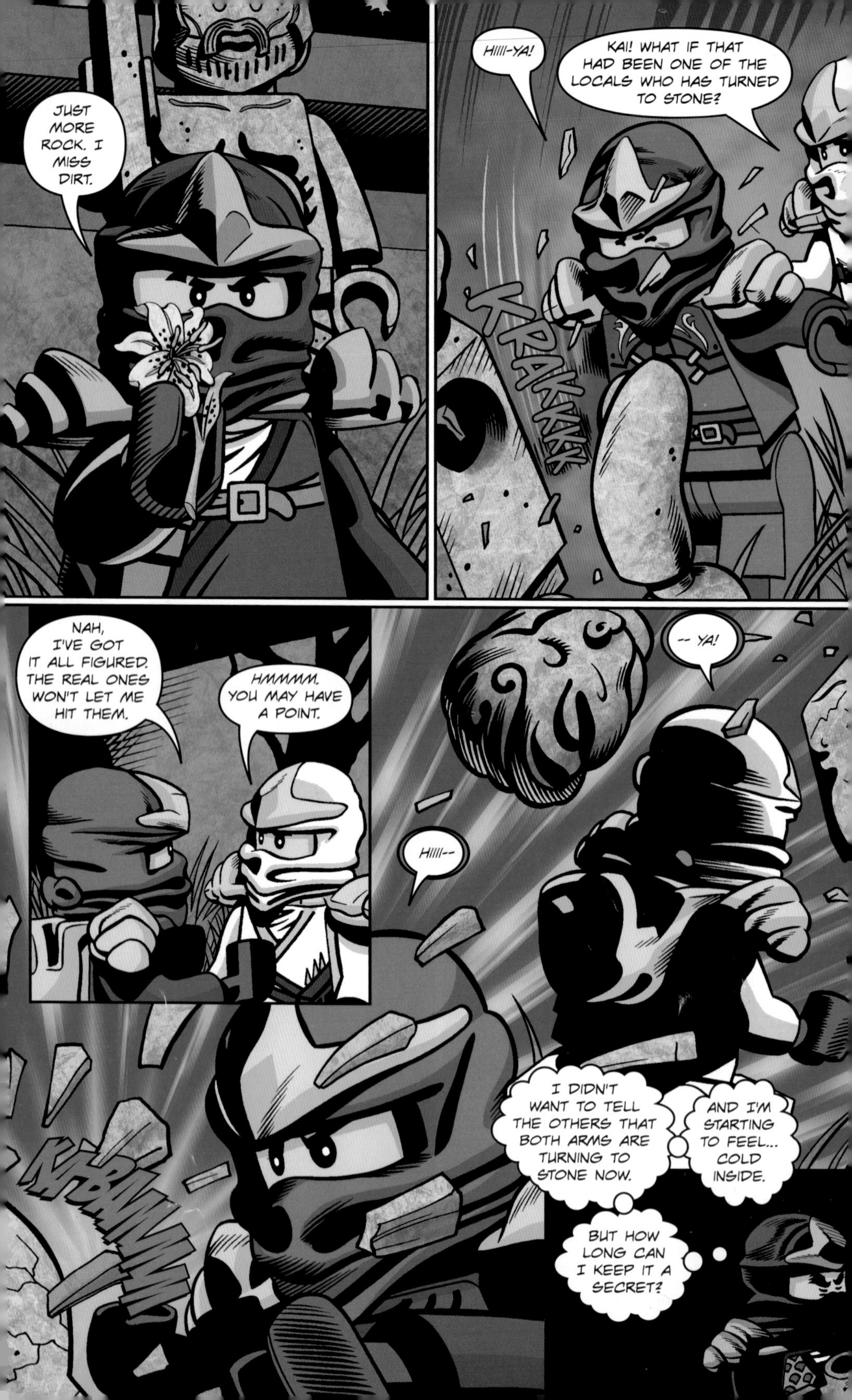
JUST MORE ROCK. I MISS DIRT.
HIIII-YA!
KAI! WHAT IF THAT HAD BEEN ONE OF THE LOCALS WHO HAS TURNED TO STONE?
KRAKKKK
NAH, I'VE GOT IT ALL FIGURED. THE REAL ONES WON'T LET ME HIT THEM.
HMMMM. YOU MAY HAVE A POINT.
-- YA!
HIIII--
I DIDN'T WANT TO TELL THE OTHERS THAT BOTH ARMS ARE TURNING TO STONE NOW.
AND I'M STARTING TO FEEL... COLD INSIDE.
BUT HOW LONG CAN I KEEP IT A SECRET?

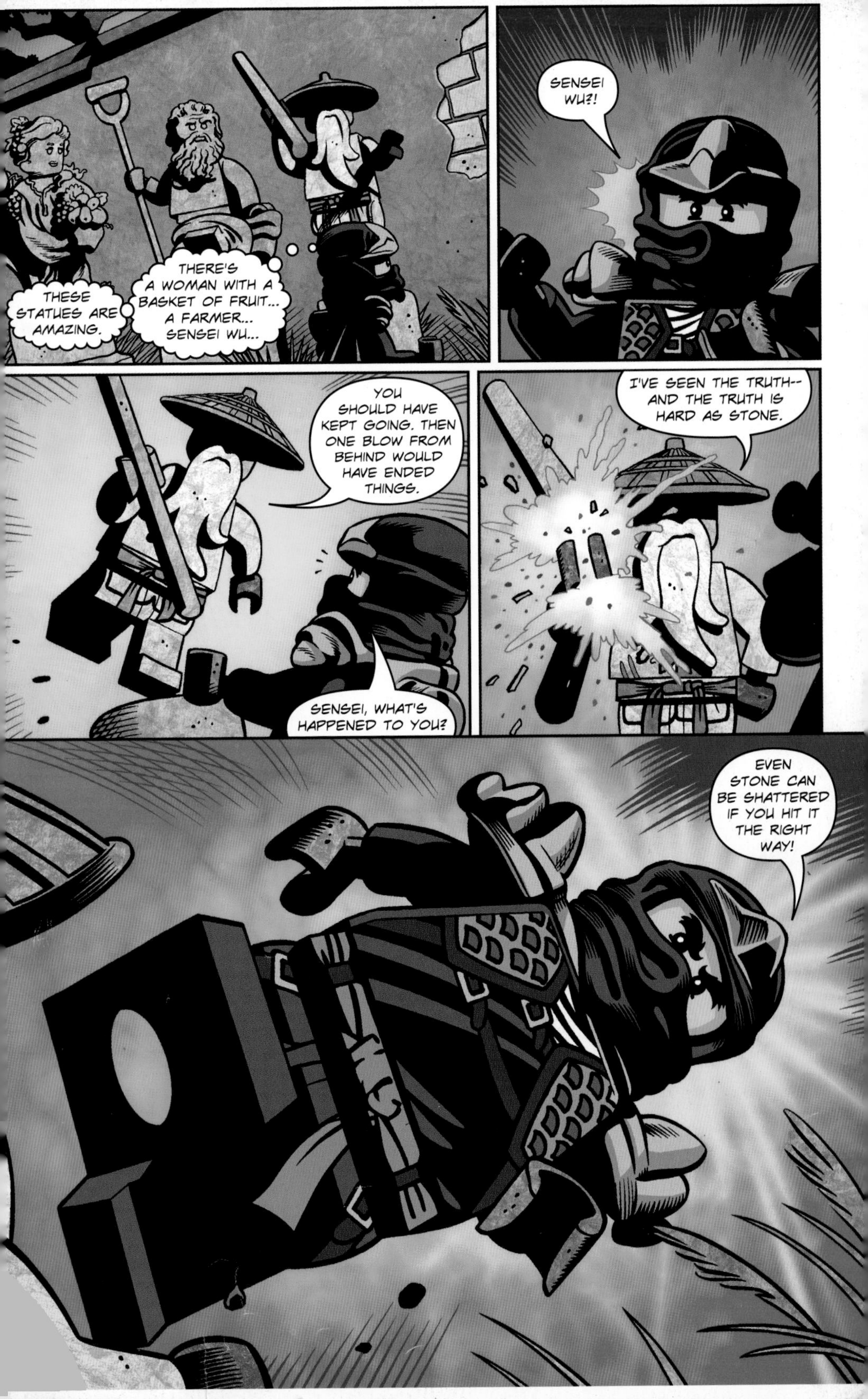
THESE STATUES ARE AMAZING.
THERE'S A WOMAN WITH A BASKET OF FRUIT... A FARMER... SENSEI WU...
SENSEI WU?!
YOU SHOULD HAVE KEPT GOING. THEN ONE BLOW FROM BEHIND WOULD HAVE ENDED THINGS.
SENSEI, WHAT'S HAPPENED TO YOU?
I'VE SEEN THE TRUTH-- AND THE TRUTH IS HARD AS STONE.
EVEN STONE CAN BE SHATTERED IF YOU HIT IT THE RIGHT WAY!

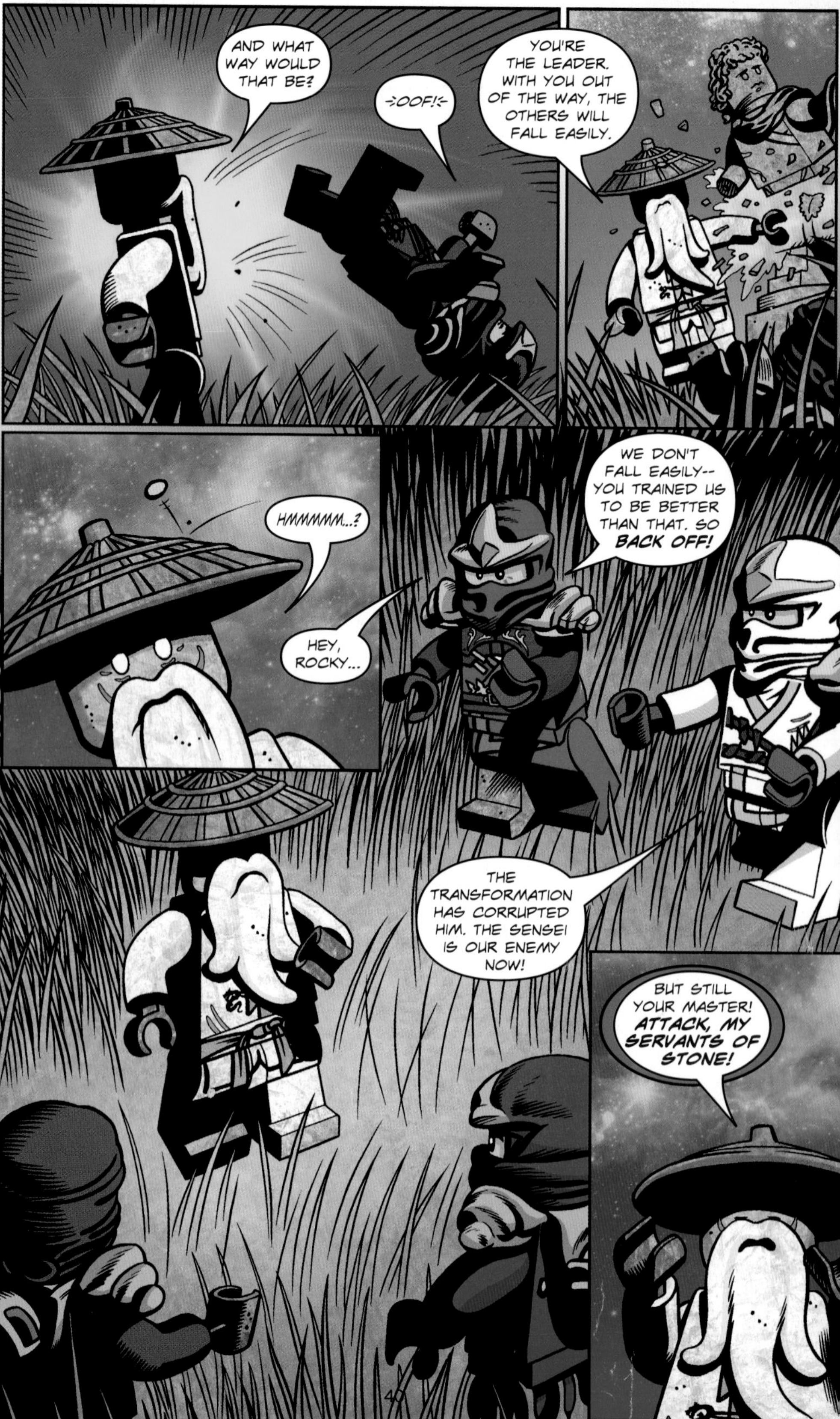
AND WHAT WAY WOULD THAT BE?
OOF!
YOU'RE THE LEADER. WITH YOU OUT OF THE WAY, THE OTHERS WILL FALL EASILY.
HMMMMM...?
HEY, ROCKY...
WE DON'T FALL EASILY-- YOU TRAINED US TO BE BETTER THAN THAT. SO **BACK OFF!**
THE TRANSFORMATION HAS CORRUPTED HIM. THE SENSEI IS OUR ENEMY NOW!
BUT STILL YOUR MASTER! ***ATTACK, MY SERVANTS OF STONE!***

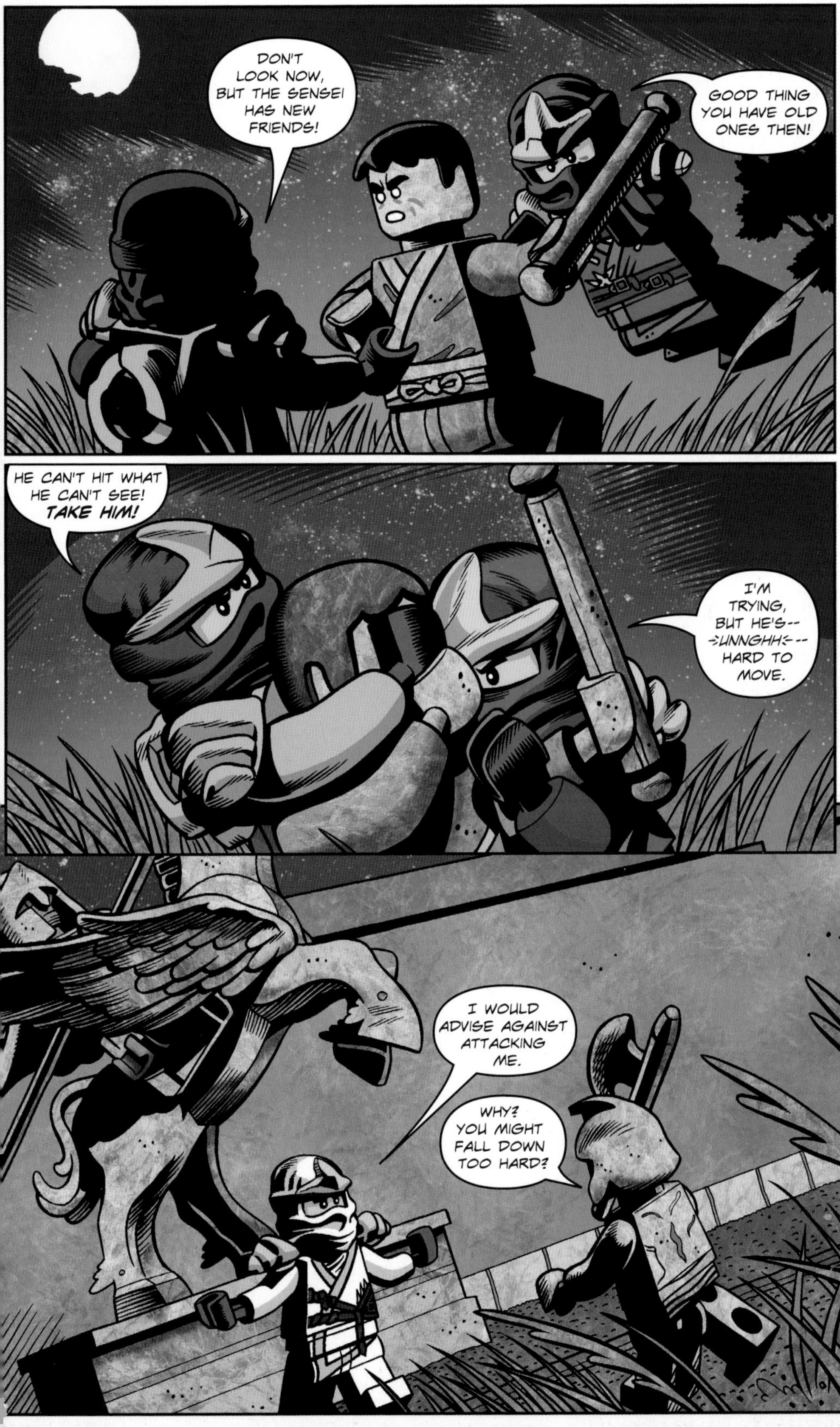
DON'T LOOK NOW, BUT THE SENSEI HAS NEW FRIENDS!
GOOD THING YOU HAVE OLD ONES THEN!
HE CAN'T HIT WHAT HE CAN'T SEE! *TAKE HIM!*
I'M TRYING, BUT HE'S-- UNNGHH-- HARD TO MOVE.
I WOULD ADVISE AGAINST ATTACKING ME.
WHY? YOU MIGHT FALL DOWN TOO HARD?

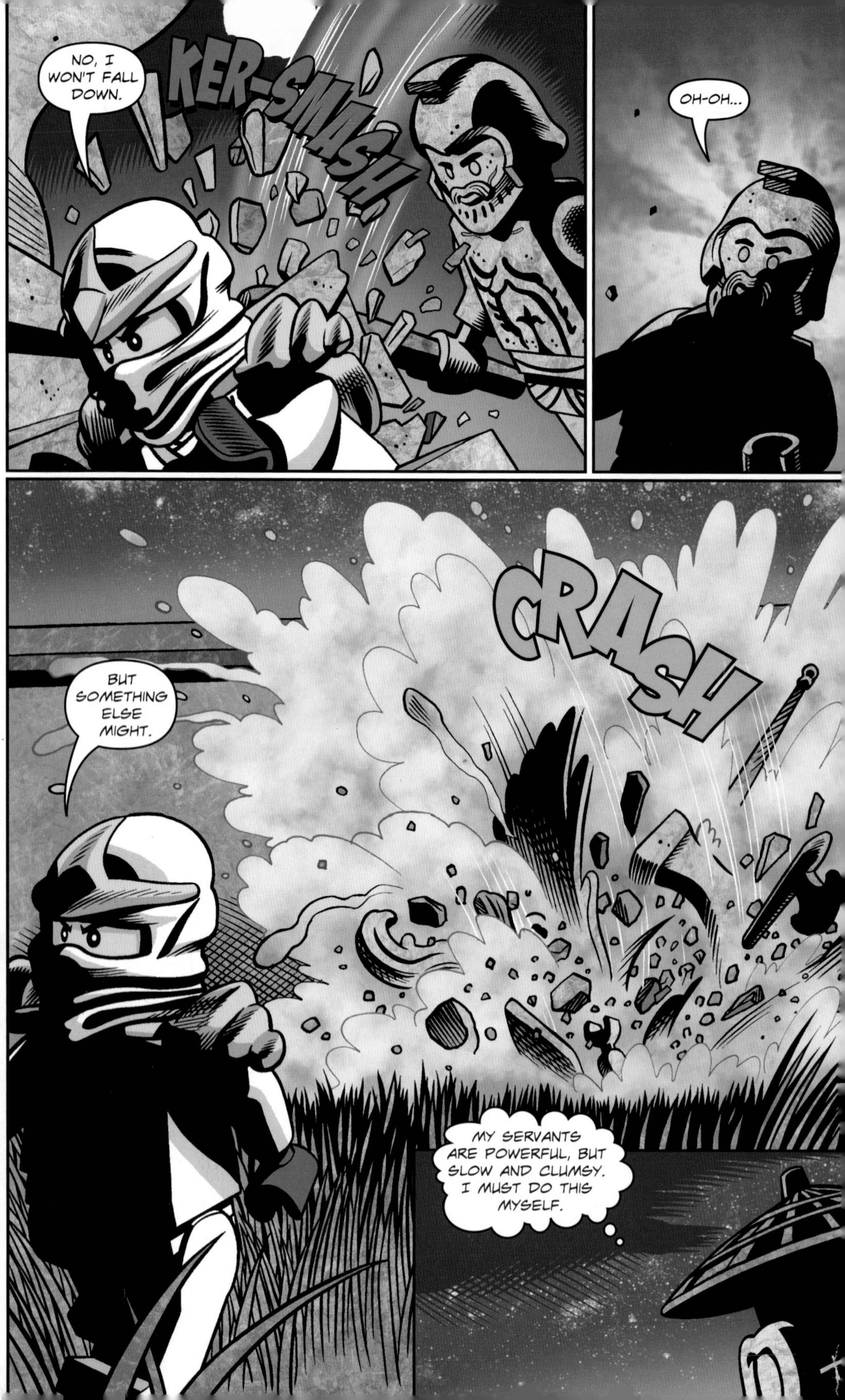
NO, I WON'T FALL DOWN.
KER-SMASH
OH-OH...
CRASH
BUT SOMETHING ELSE MIGHT.
MY SERVANTS ARE POWERFUL, BUT SLOW AND CLUMSY. I MUST DO THIS MYSELF.

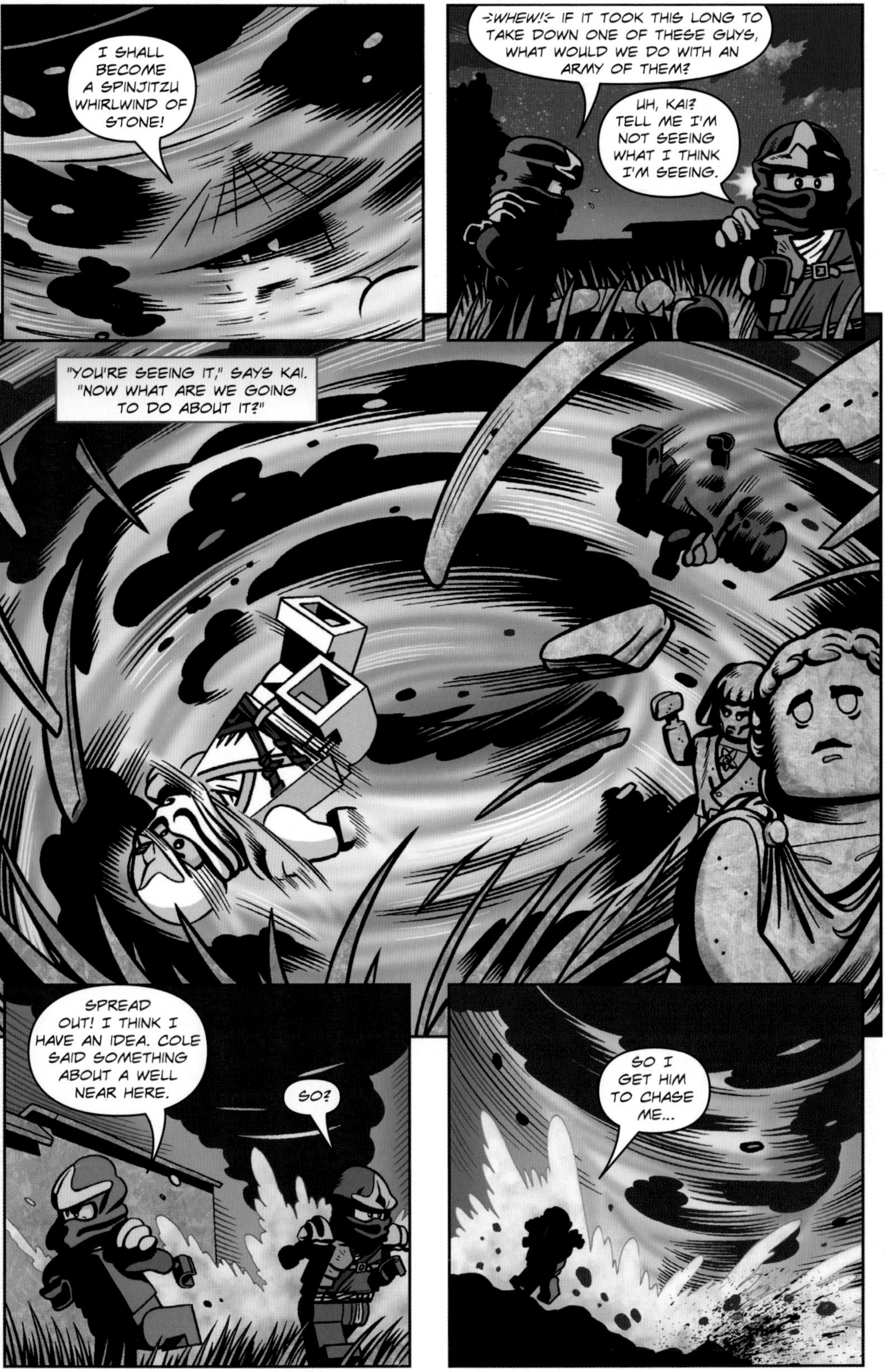

I SHALL BECOME A SPINJITZU WHIRLWIND OF STONE!
>WHEW!< IF IT TOOK THIS LONG TO TAKE DOWN ONE OF THESE GUYS, WHAT WOULD WE DO WITH AN ARMY OF THEM?
UH, KAI? TELL ME I'M NOT SEEING WHAT I THINK I'M SEEING.
"YOU'RE SEEING IT," SAYS KAI. "NOW WHAT ARE WE GOING TO DO ABOUT IT?"
SPREAD OUT! I THINK I HAVE AN IDEA. COLE SAID SOMETHING ABOUT A WELL NEAR HERE.
SO?
SO I GET HIM TO CHASE ME...

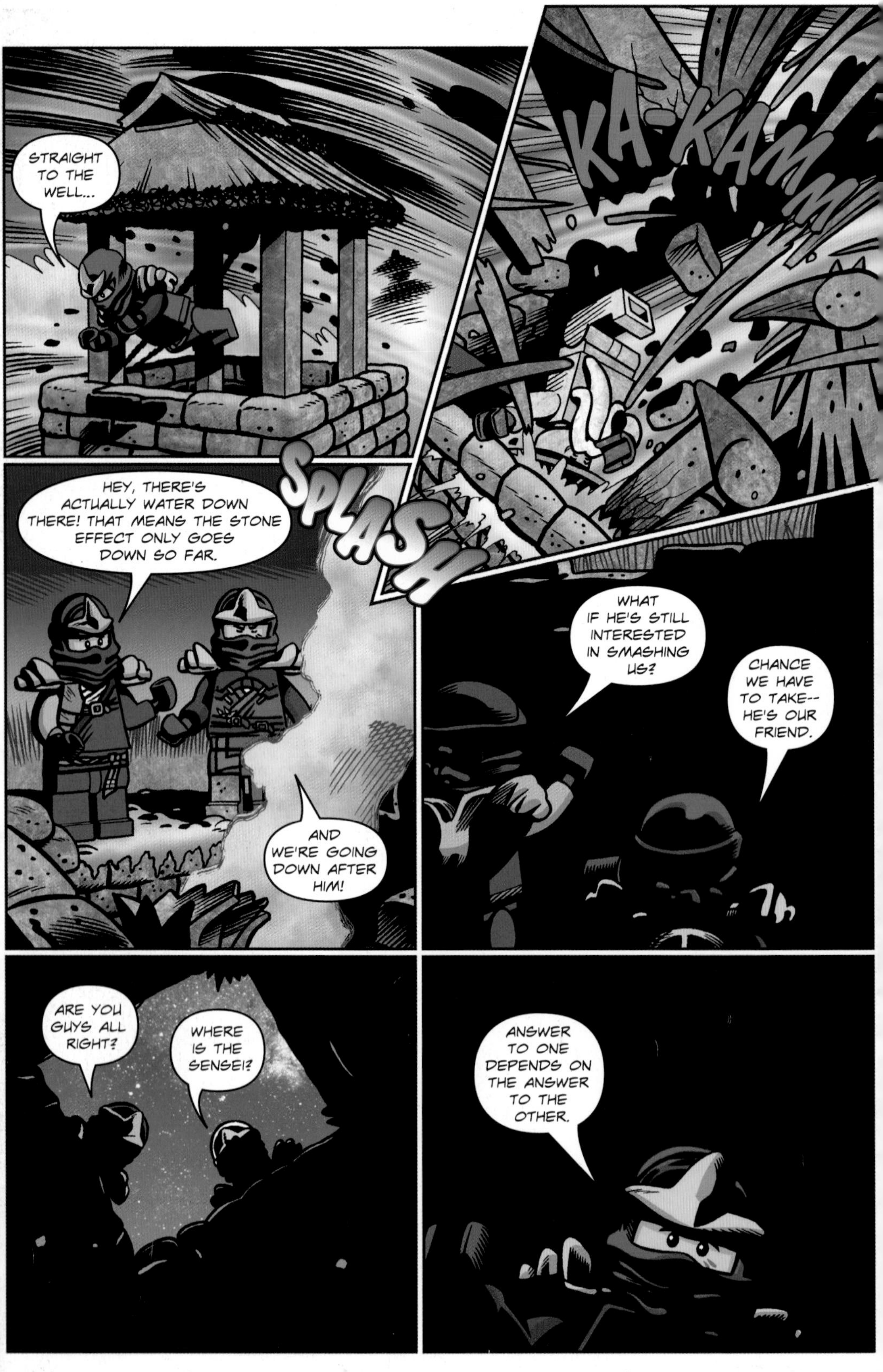
STRAIGHT TO THE WELL...
KA-KAMM
HEY, THERE'S ACTUALLY WATER DOWN THERE! THAT MEANS THE STONE EFFECT ONLY GOES DOWN SO FAR.
SPLASH
AND WE'RE GOING DOWN AFTER HIM!
WHAT IF HE'S STILL INTERESTED IN SMASHING US?
CHANCE WE HAVE TO TAKE-- HE'S OUR FRIEND.
ARE YOU GUYS ALL RIGHT?
WHERE IS THE SENSEI!?
ANSWER TO ONE DEPENDS ON THE ANSWER TO THE OTHER.

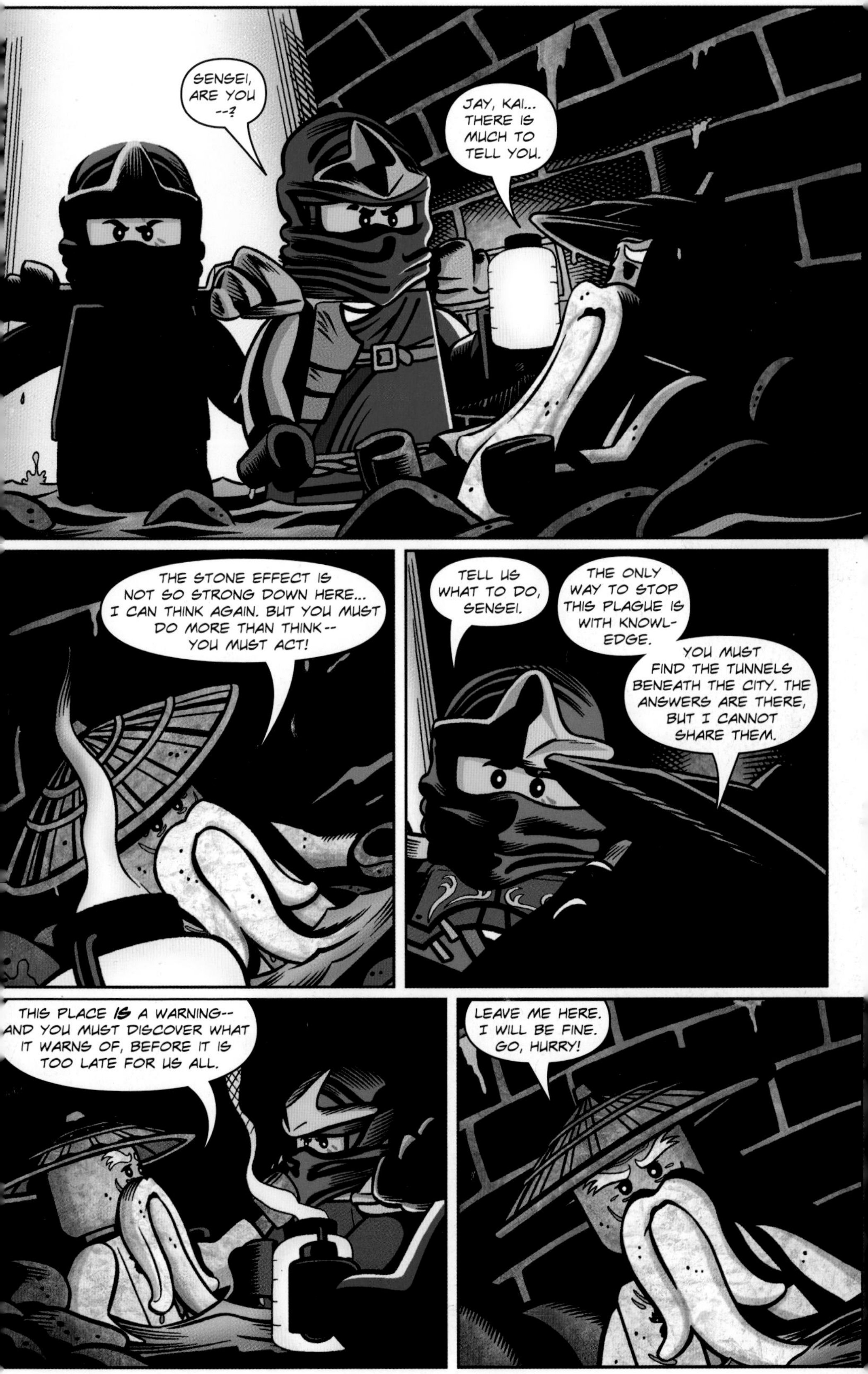
SENSEI, ARE YOU --?
JAY, KAI... THERE IS MUCH TO TELL YOU.
THE STONE EFFECT IS NOT SO STRONG DOWN HERE... I CAN THINK AGAIN. BUT YOU MUST DO MORE THAN THINK-- YOU MUST ACT!
TELL US WHAT TO DO, SENSEI.
THE ONLY WAY TO STOP THIS PLAGUE IS WITH KNOWL-EDGE.
YOU MUST FIND THE TUNNELS BENEATH THE CITY. THE ANSWERS ARE THERE, BUT I CANNOT SHARE THEM.
THIS PLACE IS A WARNING-- AND YOU MUST DISCOVER WHAT IT WARNS OF, BEFORE IT IS TOO LATE FOR US ALL.
LEAVE ME HERE. I WILL BE FINE. GO, HURRY!

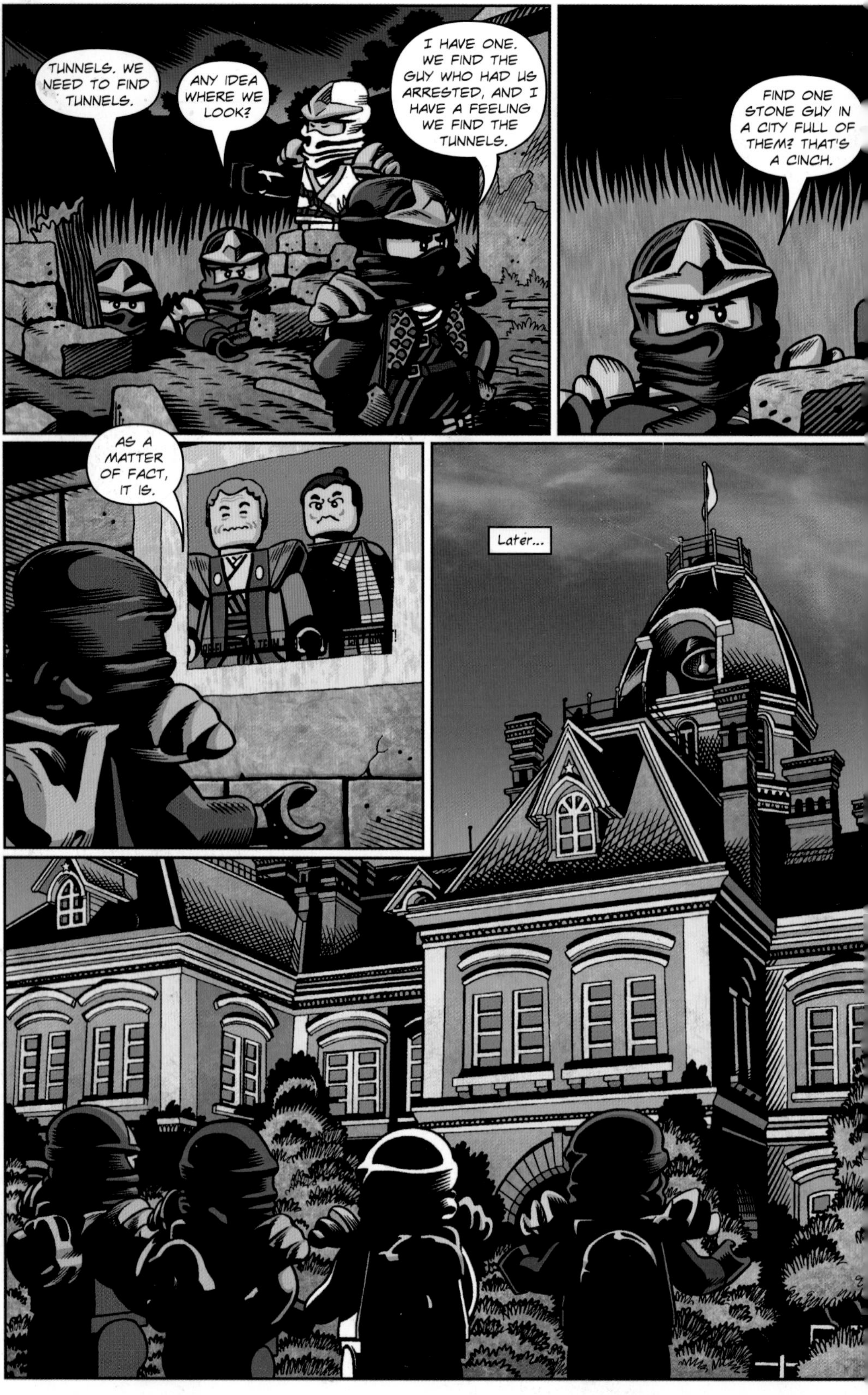
TUNNELS. WE NEED TO FIND TUNNELS.
ANY IDEA WHERE WE LOOK?
I HAVE ONE. WE FIND THE GUY WHO HAD US ARRESTED, AND I HAVE A FEELING WE FIND THE TUNNELS.
FIND ONE STONE GUY IN A CITY FULL OF THEM? THAT'S A CINCH.
AS A MATTER OF FACT, IT IS.
Later...

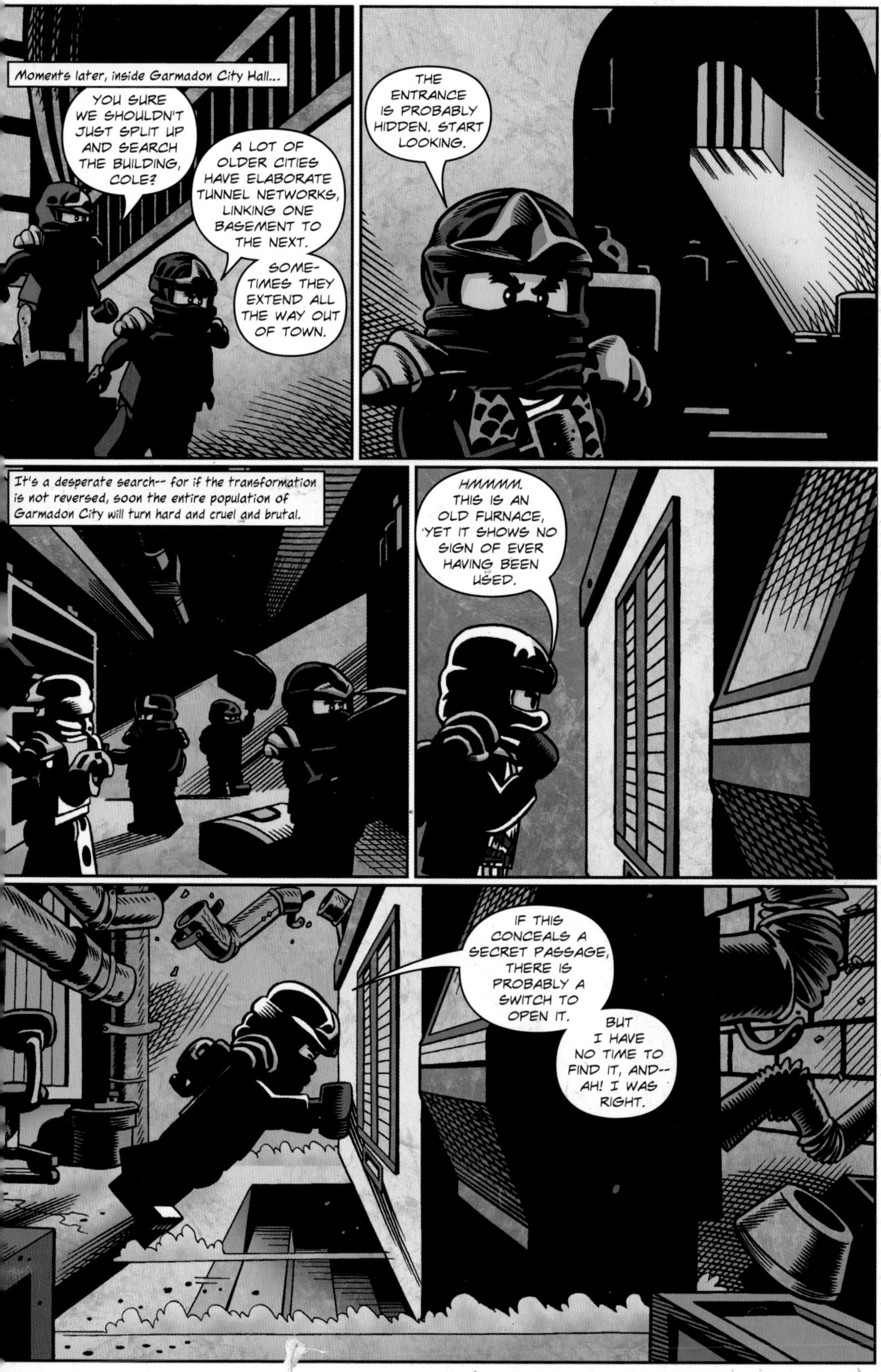
Moments later, inside Garmadon City Hall...
YOU SURE WE SHOULDN'T JUST SPLIT UP AND SEARCH THE BUILDING, COLE?
A LOT OF OLDER CITIES HAVE ELABORATE TUNNEL NETWORKS, LINKING ONE BASEMENT TO THE NEXT.
SOME-TIMES THEY EXTEND ALL THE WAY OUT OF TOWN.
THE ENTRANCE IS PROBABLY HIDDEN. START LOOKING.
It's a desperate search-- for if the transformation is not reversed, soon the entire population of Garmadon City will turn hard and cruel and brutal.
HMMMM. THIS IS AN OLD FURNACE, YET IT SHOWS NO SIGN OF EVER HAVING BEEN USED.
IF THIS CONCEALS A SECRET PASSAGE, THERE IS PROBABLY A SWITCH TO OPEN IT.
BUT I HAVE NO TIME TO FIND IT, AND-- AH! I WAS RIGHT.

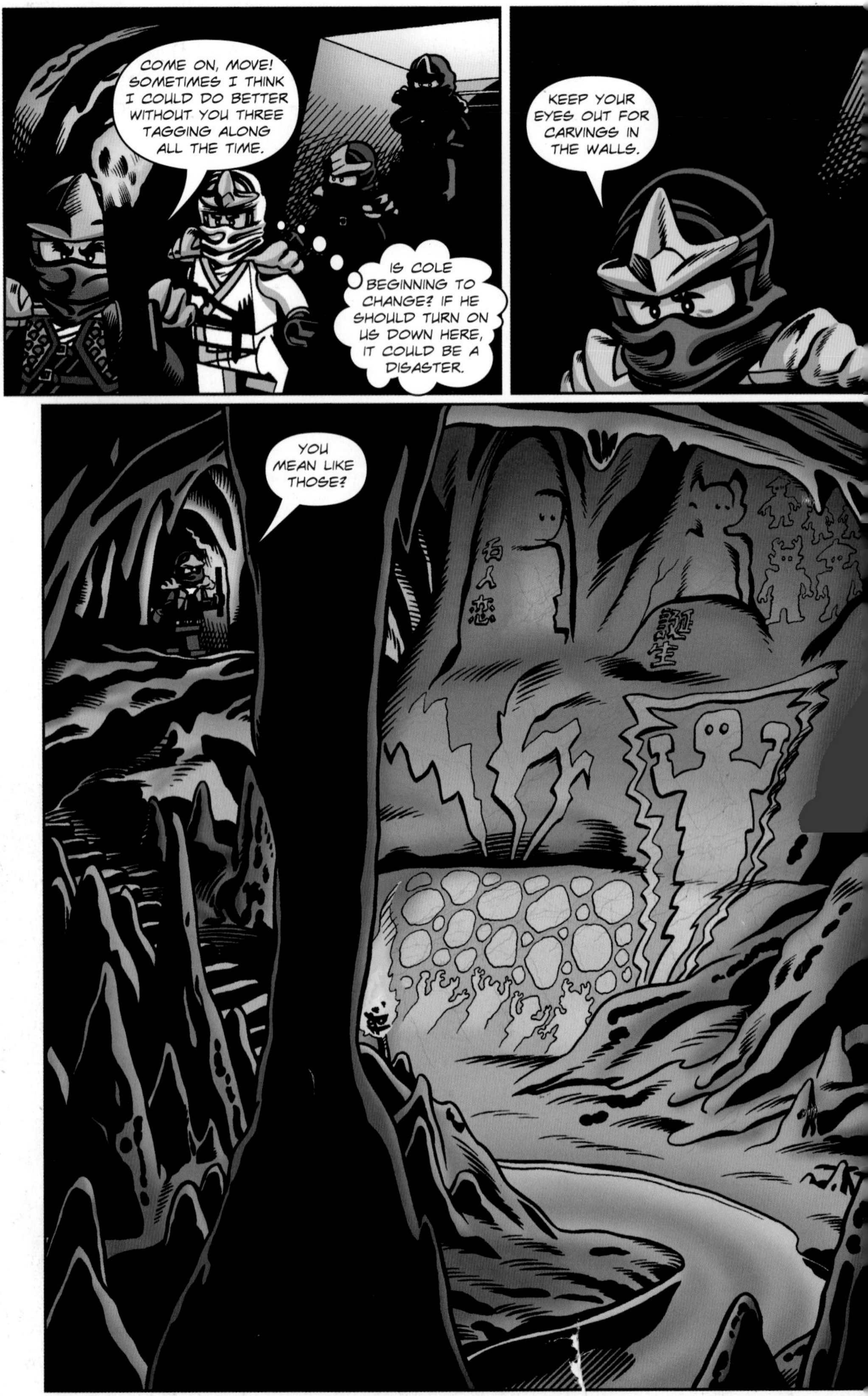
COME ON, MOVE! SOMETIMES I THINK I COULD DO BETTER WITHOUT YOU THREE TAGGING ALONG ALL THE TIME.
IS COLE BEGINNING TO CHANGE? IF HE SHOULD TURN ON US DOWN HERE, IT COULD BE A DISASTER.
KEEP YOUR EYES OUT FOR CARVINGS IN THE WALLS.
YOU MEAN LIKE THOSE?

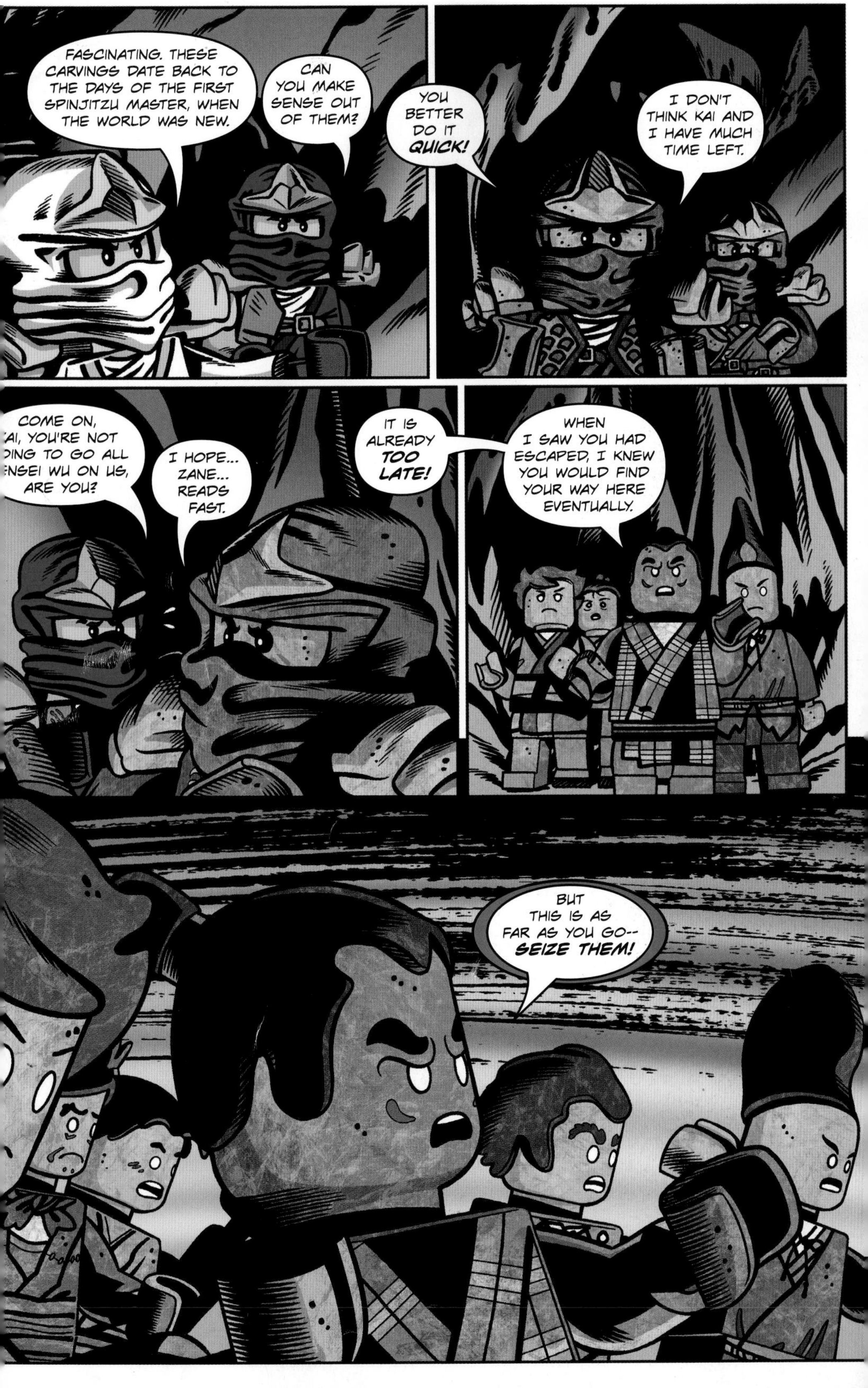
FASCINATING. THESE CARVINGS DATE BACK TO THE DAYS OF THE FIRST SPINJITZU MASTER, WHEN THE WORLD WAS NEW.
CAN YOU MAKE SENSE OUT OF THEM?
YOU BETTER DO IT QUICK!
I DON'T THINK KAI AND I HAVE MUCH TIME LEFT.
COME ON, AI, YOU'RE NOT OING TO GO ALL ENSEI WU ON US, ARE YOU?
I HOPE... ZANE... READS FAST.
IT IS ALREADY TOO LATE!
WHEN I SAW YOU HAD ESCAPED, I KNEW YOU WOULD FIND YOUR WAY HERE EVENTUALLY.
BUT THIS IS AS FAR AS YOU GO-- SEIZE THEM!

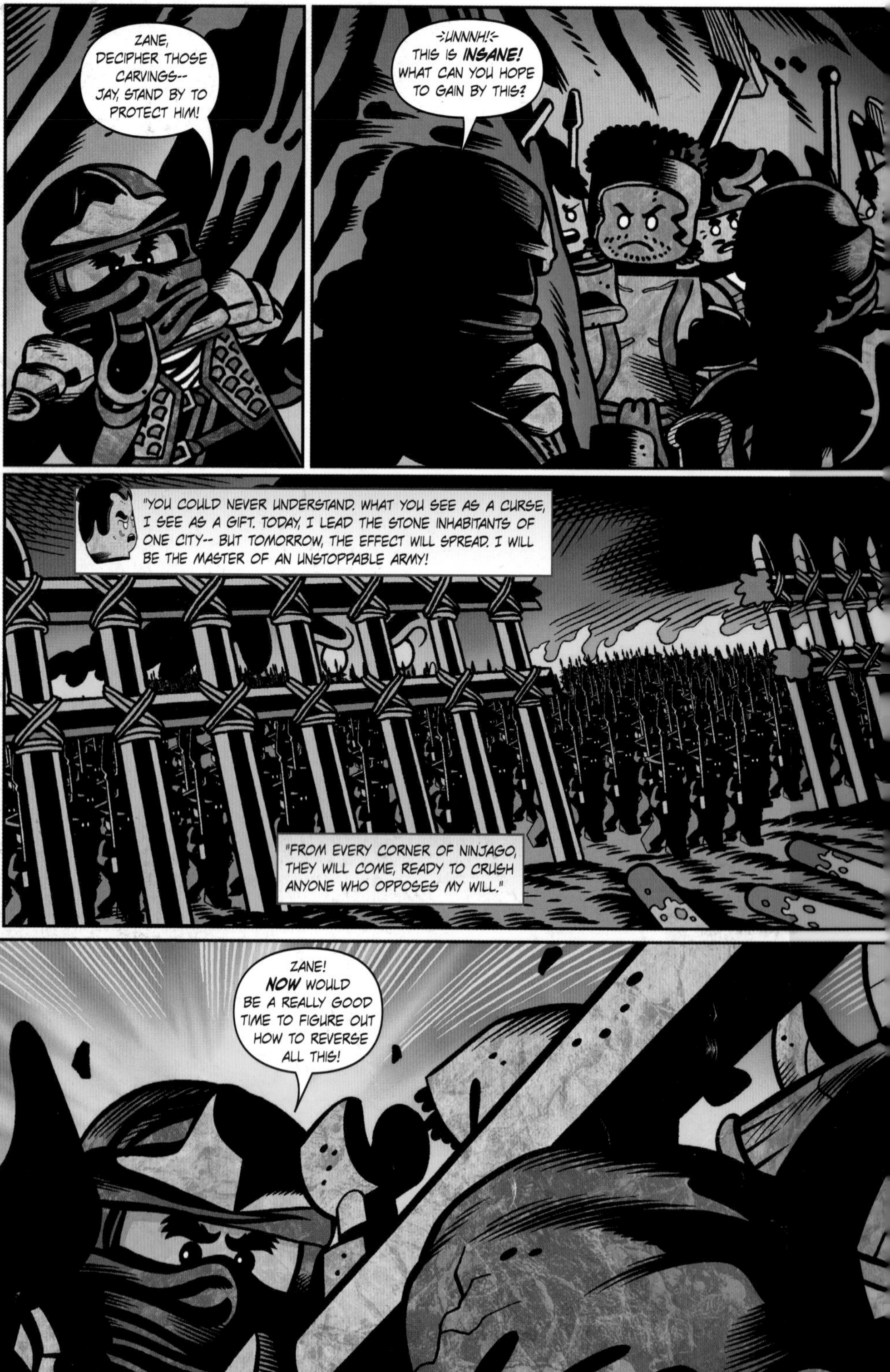
ZANE, DECIPHER THOSE CARVINGS-- JAY, STAND BY TO PROTECT HIM!
-UNNNH!- THIS IS INSANE! WHAT CAN YOU HOPE TO GAIN BY THIS?
"YOU COULD NEVER UNDERSTAND. WHAT YOU SEE AS A CURSE, I SEE AS A GIFT. TODAY, I LEAD THE STONE INHABITANTS OF ONE CITY-- BUT TOMORROW, THE EFFECT WILL SPREAD. I WILL BE THE MASTER OF AN UNSTOPPABLE ARMY!
"FROM EVERY CORNER OF NINJAGO, THEY WILL COME, READY TO CRUSH ANYONE WHO OPPOSES MY WILL."
ZANE! NOW WOULD BE A REALLY GOOD TIME TO FIGURE OUT HOW TO REVERSE ALL THIS!

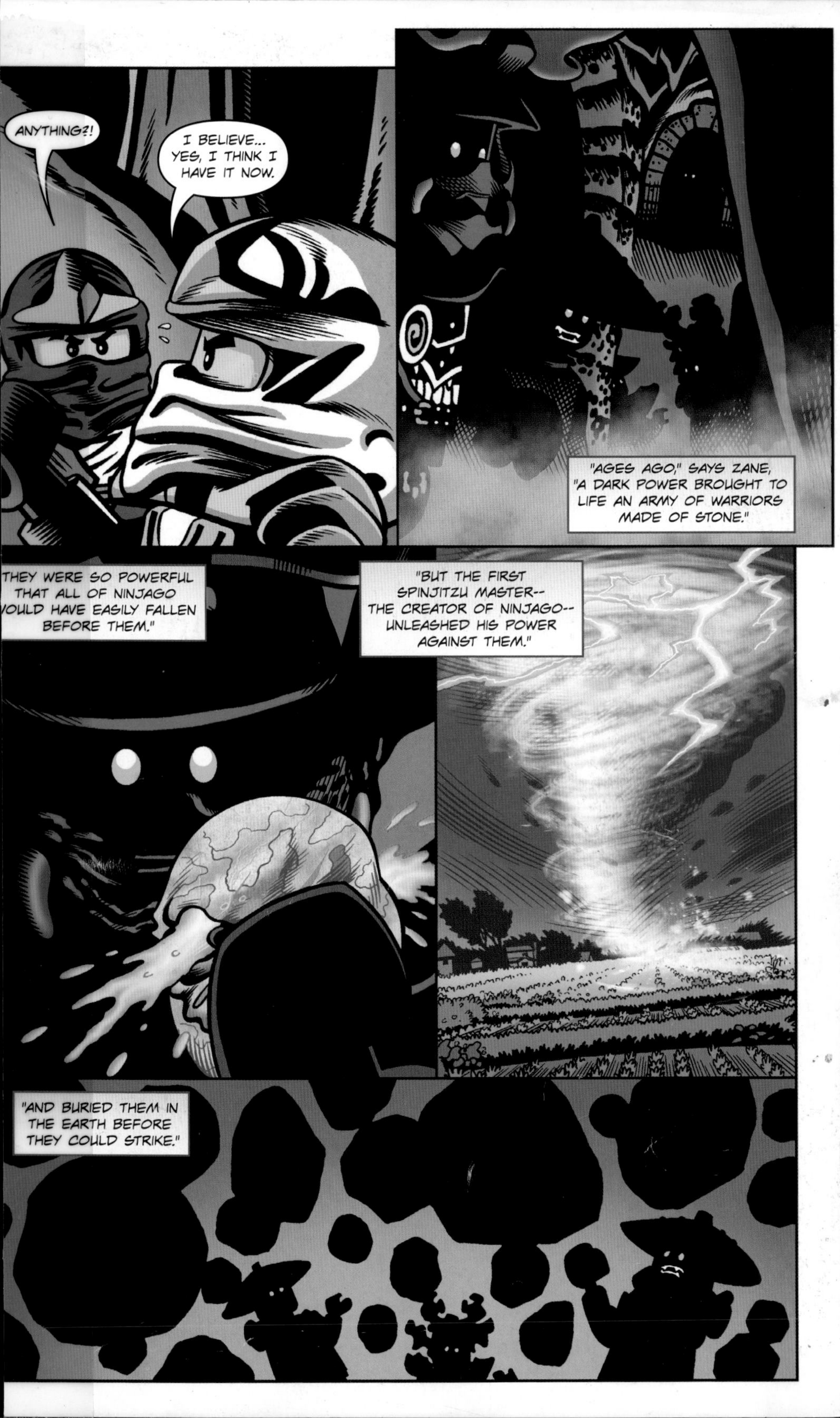

ANYTHING?!
I BELIEVE... YES, I THINK I HAVE IT NOW.
"AGES AGO," SAYS ZANE, "A DARK POWER BROUGHT TO LIFE AN ARMY OF WARRIORS MADE OF STONE."
THEY WERE SO POWERFUL THAT ALL OF NINJAGO WOULD HAVE EASILY FALLEN BEFORE THEM."
"BUT THE FIRST SPINJITZU MASTER-- THE CREATOR OF NINJAGO-- UNLEASHED HIS POWER AGAINST THEM."
"AND BURIED THEM IN THE EARTH BEFORE THEY COULD STRIKE."

THAT'S IT-- STONE WARRIORS! THAT IS WHAT THE WARNING IS ABOUT. IT MUST BE!

I HOPE THERE'S MORE TO IT THAN THAT, BECAUSE DON'T LOOK NOW, BUT YOUR BIG REVELATION--

"IT HASN'T CHANGED ANYTHING," SAYS JAY.

WAIT, WHAT'S THIS? THERE IS MORE TO THE CARVING, BUT IT'S HIDDEN.

PERHAPS THE FINAL ANSWER IS HERE...

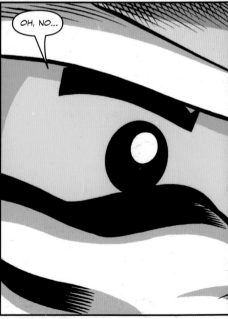

OH, NO...

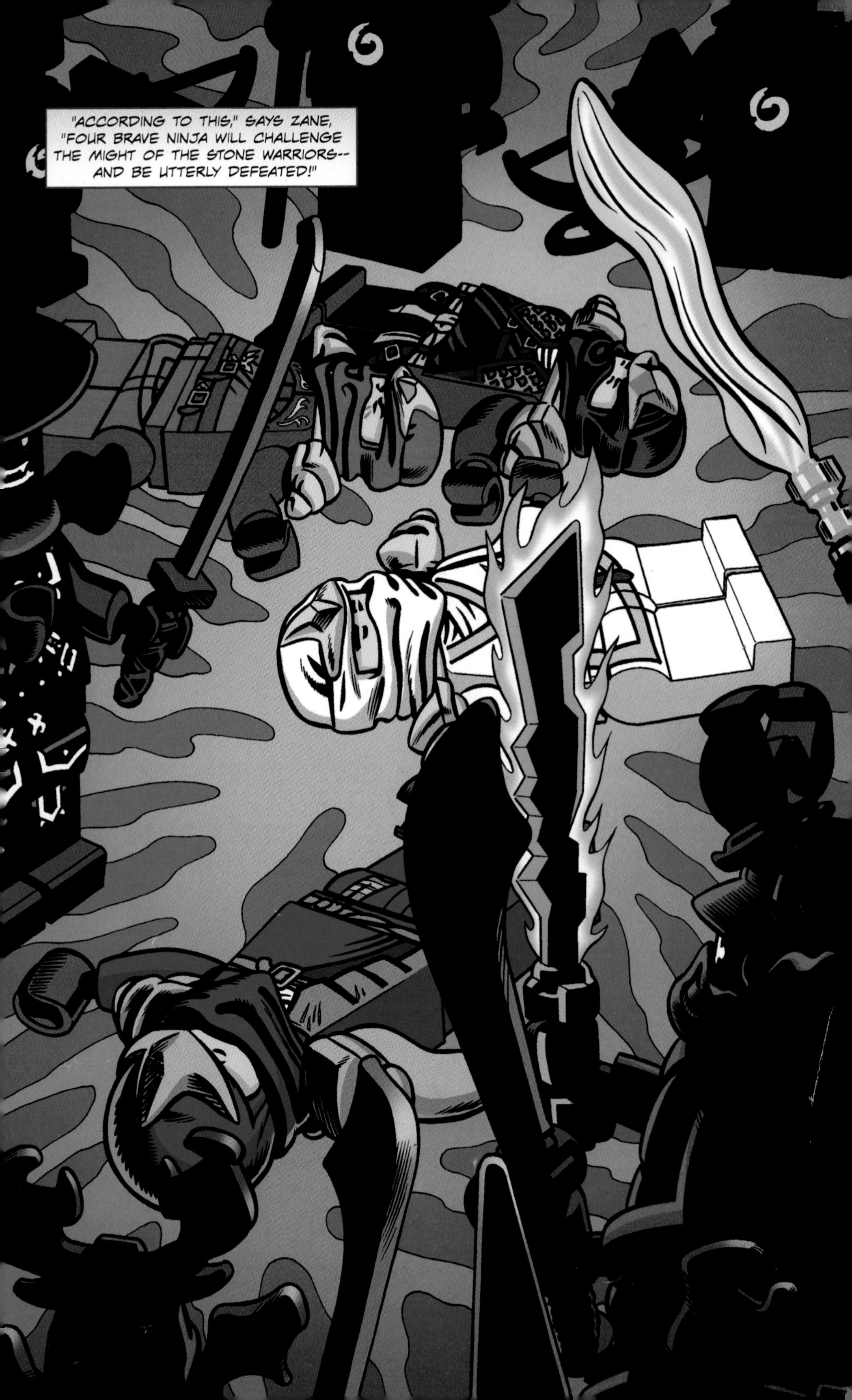
"ACCORDING TO THIS," SAYS ZANE, "FOUR BRAVE NINJA WILL CHALLENGE THE MIGHT OF THE STONE WARRIORS-- AND BE UTTERLY DEFEATED!"

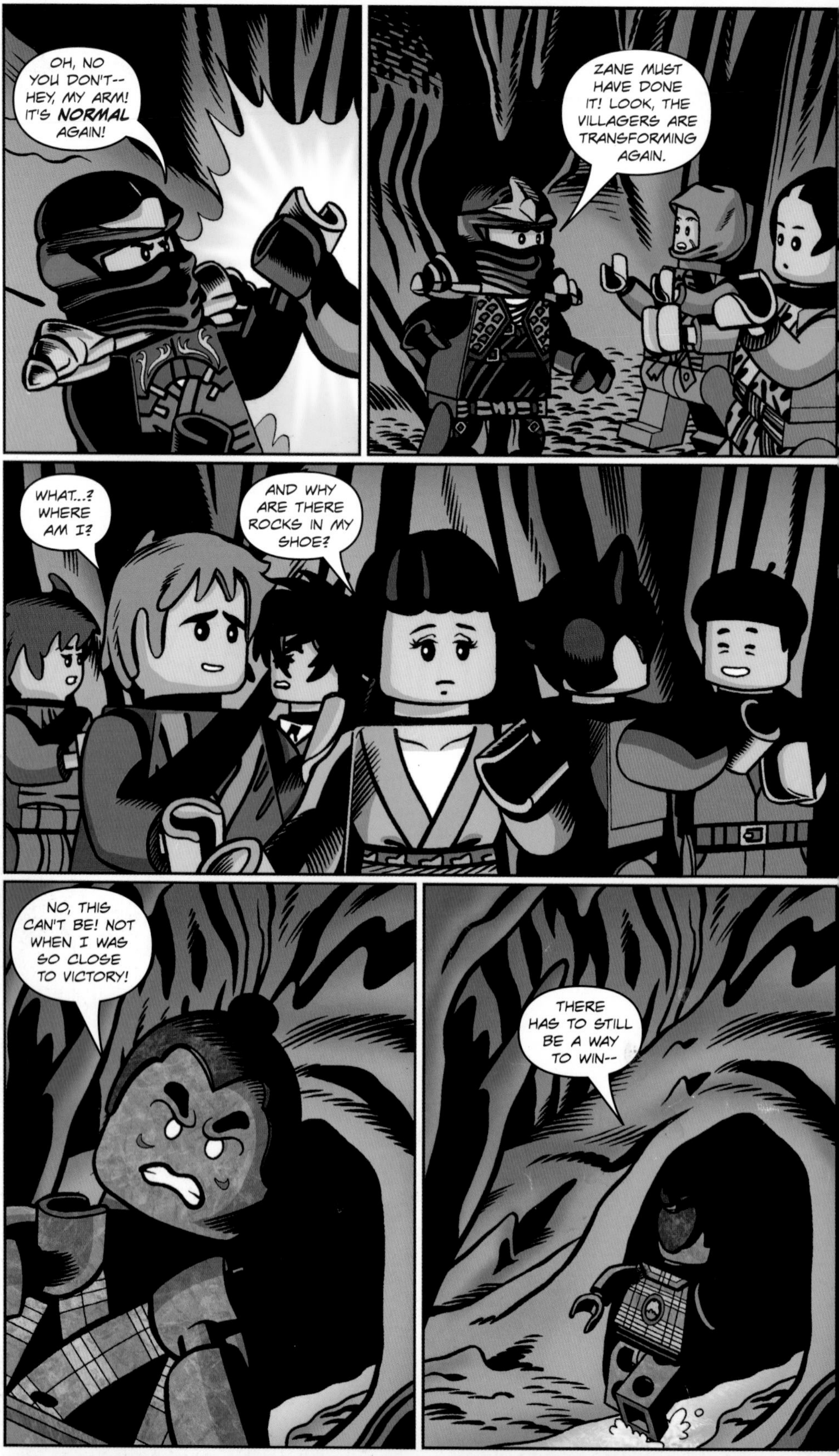
OH, NO YOU DON'T-- HEY, MY ARM! IT'S NORMAL AGAIN!
ZANE MUST HAVE DONE IT! LOOK, THE VILLAGERS ARE TRANSFORMING AGAIN.
WHAT...? WHERE AM I?
AND WHY ARE THERE ROCKS IN MY SHOE?
NO, THIS CAN'T BE! NOT WHEN I WAS SO CLOSE TO VICTORY!
THERE HAS TO STILL BE A WAY TO WIN--

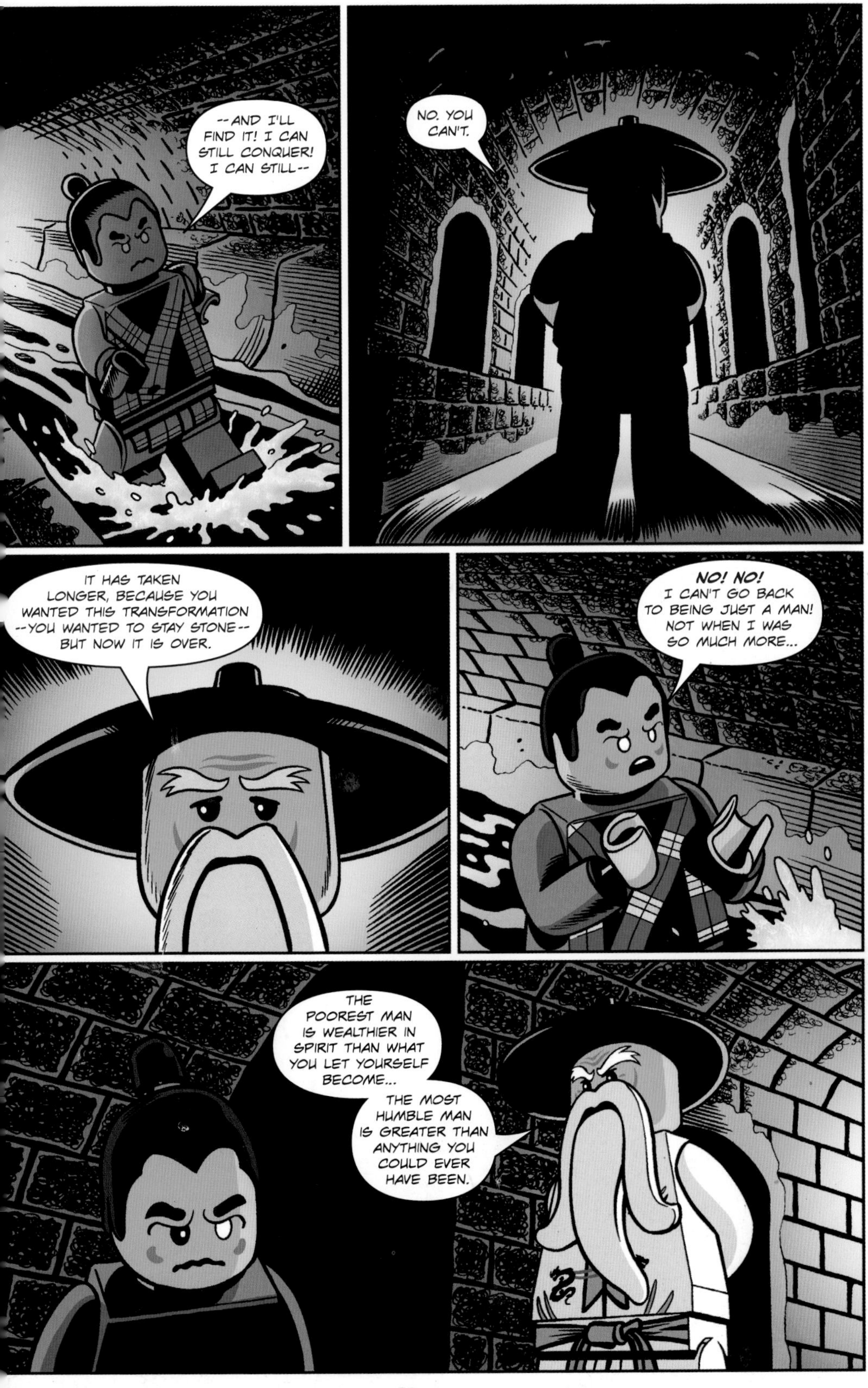
--AND I'LL FIND IT! I CAN STILL CONQUER! I CAN STILL--
NO. YOU CAN'T.
IT HAS TAKEN LONGER, BECAUSE YOU WANTED THIS TRANSFORMATION --YOU WANTED TO STAY STONE-- BUT NOW IT IS OVER.
NO! NO! I CAN'T GO BACK TO BEING JUST A MAN! NOT WHEN I WAS SO MUCH MORE...
THE POOREST MAN IS WEALTHIER IN SPIRIT THAN WHAT YOU LET YOURSELF BECOME...
THE MOST HUMBLE MAN IS GREATER THAN ANYTHING YOU COULD EVER HAVE BEEN.

Morning comes to Garmadon City, where the only things made of rock... are rocks.

SO IT REALLY WAS JUST LIKE YOUR OLD CASE, SENSEI?

IN A SENSE, YES.

THE PRESENCE OF THE ICE WORMS CAUSED EVERYTHING AROUND TO FREEZE, AS NATURE REBELLED AGAINST CREATURES WHO HAD NO BUSINESS WHERE THEY WERE.

"AND, HERE, NATURE CAUSED ALL THINGS TO TURN TO ROCK AS A WARNING ABOUT THE STONE WARRIORS AND THE THREAT THEY REPRESENT"

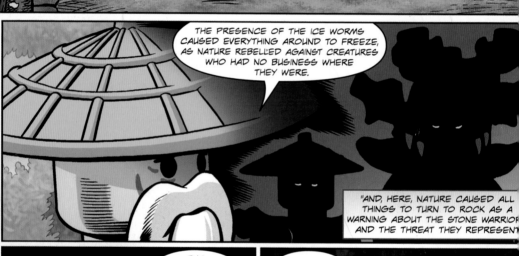

BUT IF THE STONE WARRIORS WERE BURIED BY THE FIRST SPINJITZU MASTER, WHAT IS THERE TO BE WORRIED ABOUT?

BURYING SOMETHING IS ONE THING... HAVING IT STAY BURIED IS QUITE ANOTHER.

56

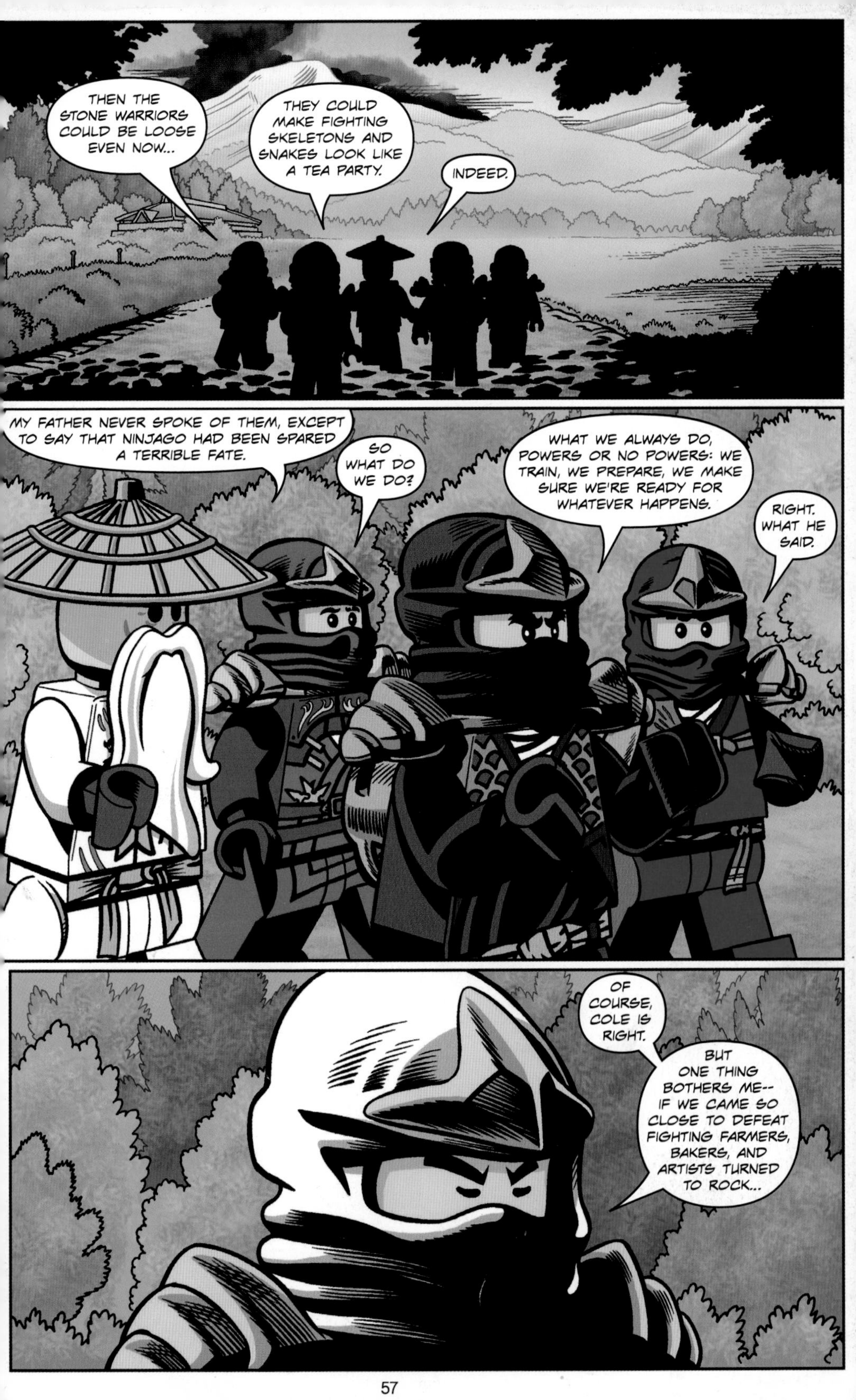
THEN THE STONE WARRIORS COULD BE LOOSE EVEN NOW...
THEY COULD MAKE FIGHTING SKELETONS AND SNAKES LOOK LIKE A TEA PARTY.
INDEED.
MY FATHER NEVER SPOKE OF THEM, EXCEPT TO SAY THAT NINJAGO HAD BEEN SPARED A TERRIBLE FATE.
SO WHAT DO WE DO?
WHAT WE ALWAYS DO, POWERS OR NO POWERS: WE TRAIN, WE PREPARE, WE MAKE SURE WE'RE READY FOR WHATEVER HAPPENS.
RIGHT. WHAT HE SAID.
OF COURSE, COLE IS RIGHT.
BUT ONE THING BOTHERS ME-- IF WE CAME SO CLOSE TO DEFEAT FIGHTING FARMERS, BAKERS, AND ARTISTS TURNED TO ROCK...

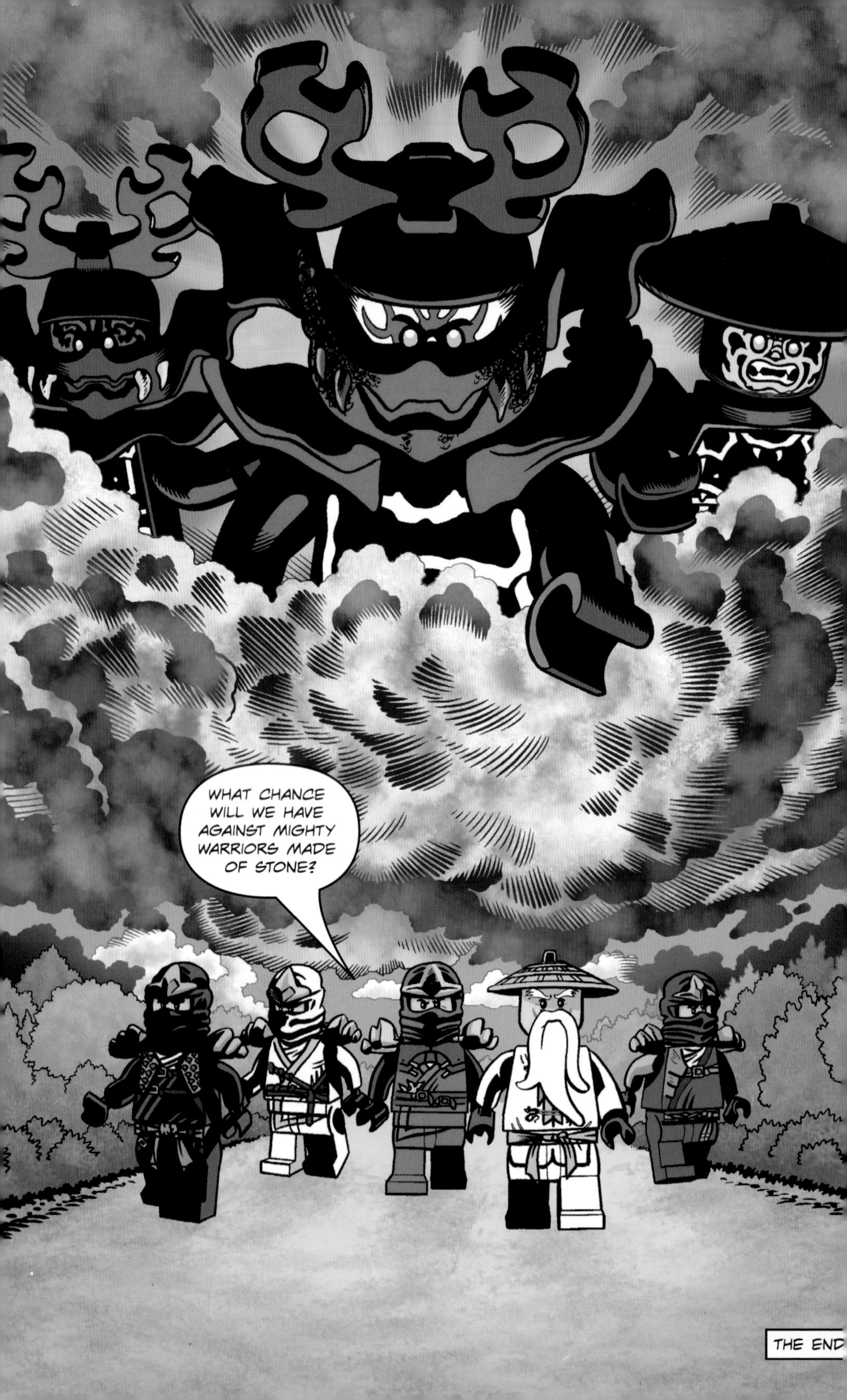
WHAT CHANCE WILL WE HAVE AGAINST MIGHTY WARRIORS MADE OF STONE?
THE END

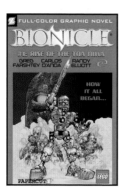

LEGO® GRAPHIC NOVELS AVAILABLE FROM PAPERCUTZ™

FULL-COLOR GRAPHIC NOVEL
BIONICLE
#1: RISE OF THE TOA NUVA
GREG FARSHTEY CARLOS D'ANDA RANDY ELLIOTT
HOW IT ALL BEGAN...
PAPERCUTZ
LEGO

BIONICLE #1

FULL-COLOR GRAPHIC NOVEL
BIONICLE
#2: CHALLENGE OF THE RAKSHI
GREG FARSHTEY RANDY ELLIOTT
PAPERCUTZ
LEGO

BIONICLE #2

FULL-COLOR GRAPHIC NOVEL
BIONICLE
#3: CITY OF LEGENDS
GREG FARSHTEY RANDY ELLIOTT
PAPERCUTZ
LEGO

BIONICLE #3

FULL-COLOR GRAPHIC NOVEL
BIONICLE
#4: TRIAL BY FIRE
GREG FARSHTEY RANDY ELLIOTT
PAPERCUTZ
LEGO

BIONICLE #4

FULL-COLOR GRAPHIC NOVEL
BIONICLE
#5: THE BATTLE OF VOYA NUI
GREG FARSHTEY STUART SAYGER
PAPERCUTZ
LEGO

BIONICLE #5

FEATURING HYDRAXON IN AN ALL-NEW STORY!
FULL-COLOR GRAPHIC NOVEL
BIONICLE
#6: THE UNDERWATER CITY
GREG FARSHTEY STUART SAYGER CHRISTIAN ZANIER
PAPERCUTZ
LEGO

BIONICLE #6

FULL-COLOR GRAPHIC NOVEL
BIONICLE
#7: REALM OF FEAR
GREG FARSHTEY LEIGH GALLAGHER
PAPERCUTZ
LEGO

BIONICLE #7

ALL-NEW! ALL-OUT AWESOME ACTION!
FULL-COLOR GRAPHIC NOVEL
BIONICLE
#8: LEGENDS OF BARA MAGNA
GREG FARSHTEY CHRISTIAN ZANIER
PAPERCUTZ
LEGO

BIONICLE #8

FULL-COLOR GRAPHIC NOVEL
BIONICLE
#9: FALL OF ATERO
GREG FARSHTEY POP MHAN
PAPERCUTZ
LEGO

BIONICLE #9

MATA NUI'S GUIDE TO BARA MAGNA
BIONICLE
GREG FARSHTEY

Mata Nui's Guide to Bara Magna

BIONICLE® graphic novels are available in paperback and hardcover at booksellers everywhere.

BIONICLE #1-3, 8, and 9 are $8.99 in paperback, $13.99 in hardcover. BIONICLE #4-7 are $7.95 in paperback and $12.95 in hardcover. Guide Books are $9.99 each in paperback only. You can also order online at www.papercutz.com. Or call 1-800-886-1223, Monday through Fridays, 9 – 5 EST. MC, Visa, and AmEx accepted. To order by mail, please add $4.00 for postage and handling for first book ordered, $1.00 for each additional book and make check payable to NBM Publishing. Send to: Papercutz, 160 Broadway, Suite 700, East Wing, New York, NY 10038.

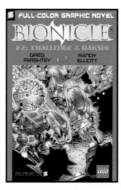

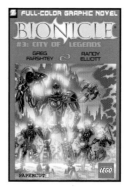

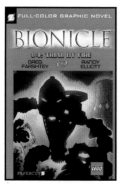

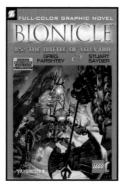

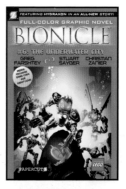

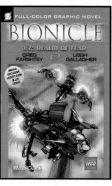

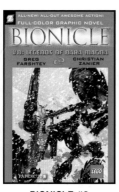

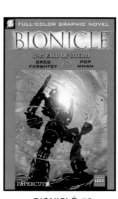

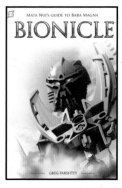

WATCH OUT FOR PAPERCUTZ™

Welcome to the virtually snake-less sixth LEGO® NINJAGO graphic novel from Papercutz, the little company dedicated to publishing great graphic novels for all ages. Of course, that's easy to do when working with such talented folks as writer Greg Farshtey, artist Jolyon Yates, colorist Jayjay Jackson, letterer Bryan Senka, and Associate Editor Michael Petranek. Don't tell Papercutz publisher Terry Nantier that with such an incredible creative crew, there's almost no need for me, Editor-in-Chief Jim Salicrup!

It seems that wherever you look these days, you're going to see LEGO® NINJAGO! It's truly LEGO NINJAGO-MANIA! In addition to the best-selling Papercutz LEGO NINJAGO graphic novels, there's also the hit LEGO NINJAGO TV series on Cartoon Network and the LEGO NINJAGO chapter books from Scholastic. Perhaps the only place you don't find LEGO NINJAGO is on toy store shelves in the LEGO section—because they sell out so fast! (Don't give up, there's more on the way!)

Lest you think I may be exaggerating (who, me?), here's a story that'll set you straight. Recently, globe-trotting LEGO NINJAGO artist Jolyon Yates was out in the country in Australia, at the remotest restaurant he's ever been to-- and for some reason, he's been to a lot of remote restaurants! Fearlessly, he walks in and sees a boy named Owen:

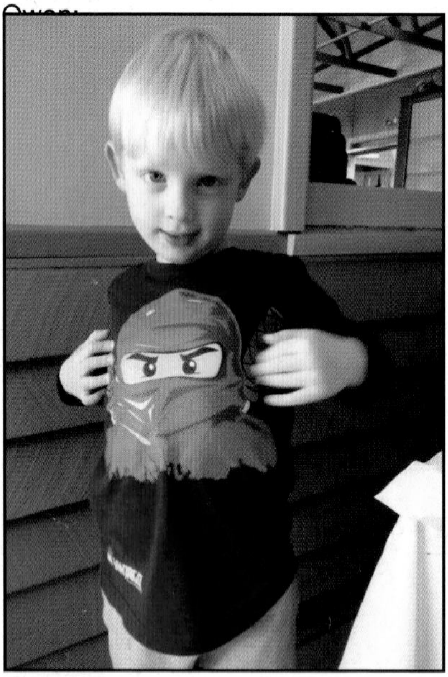

Inside the restaurant, good ol' Jolyon was soon whipping up a sketch of Kai for the young LEGO NINJAGO fan. But the story doesn't end there! Then the chef rushes out of the kitchen to tell Jolyon that he just phoned his son in Brisbane, who's also a big LEGO NINJAGO fan! Of course, Jolyon was then drawing even more LEGO NINJAGO sketches! LEGO NINJAGO-MANIA is running wild!

Fortunately, you don't need to find Mr. Yates in the Land Down Under to get great artwork from him (I, mean that could get really expensive!). You simply need to go to your favorite bookseller or library soon and ask for LEGO NINJAGO #7 "Stone Cold"! Check out the sneak preview on the following pages...

So, until next time, keep spinnin'!

Thanks,

Jim

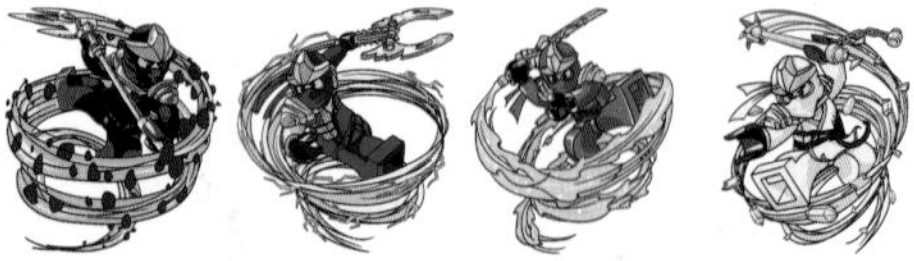

STAY IN TOUCH!

EMAIL:	salicrup@papercutz.com
WEB:	www.papercutz.com
TWITTER:	@papercutzgn
FACEBOOK:	PAPERCUTZGRAPHICNOVELS
FAN MAIL:	Papercutz, 160 Broadway, Suite 700, East Wing, New York, NY 10038

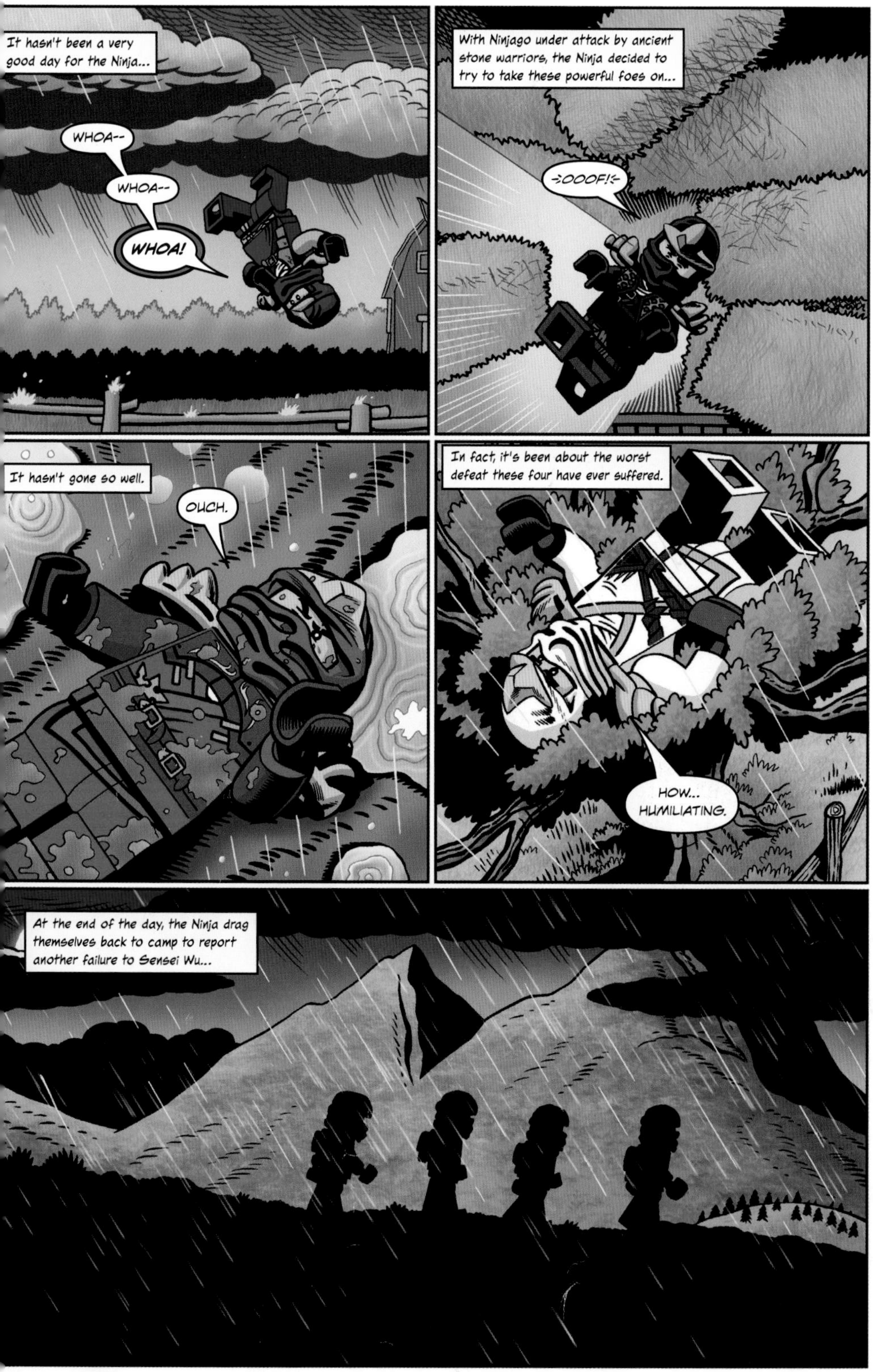
It hasn't been a very good day for the Ninja...
WHOA--
WHOA--
WHOA!
With Ninjago under attack by ancient stone warriors, the Ninja decided to try to take these powerful foes on...
OOOF!
It hasn't gone so well.
OUCH.
In fact, it's been about the worst defeat these four have ever suffered.
HOW... HUMILIATING.
At the end of the day, the Ninja drag themselves back to camp to report another failure to Sensei Wu...

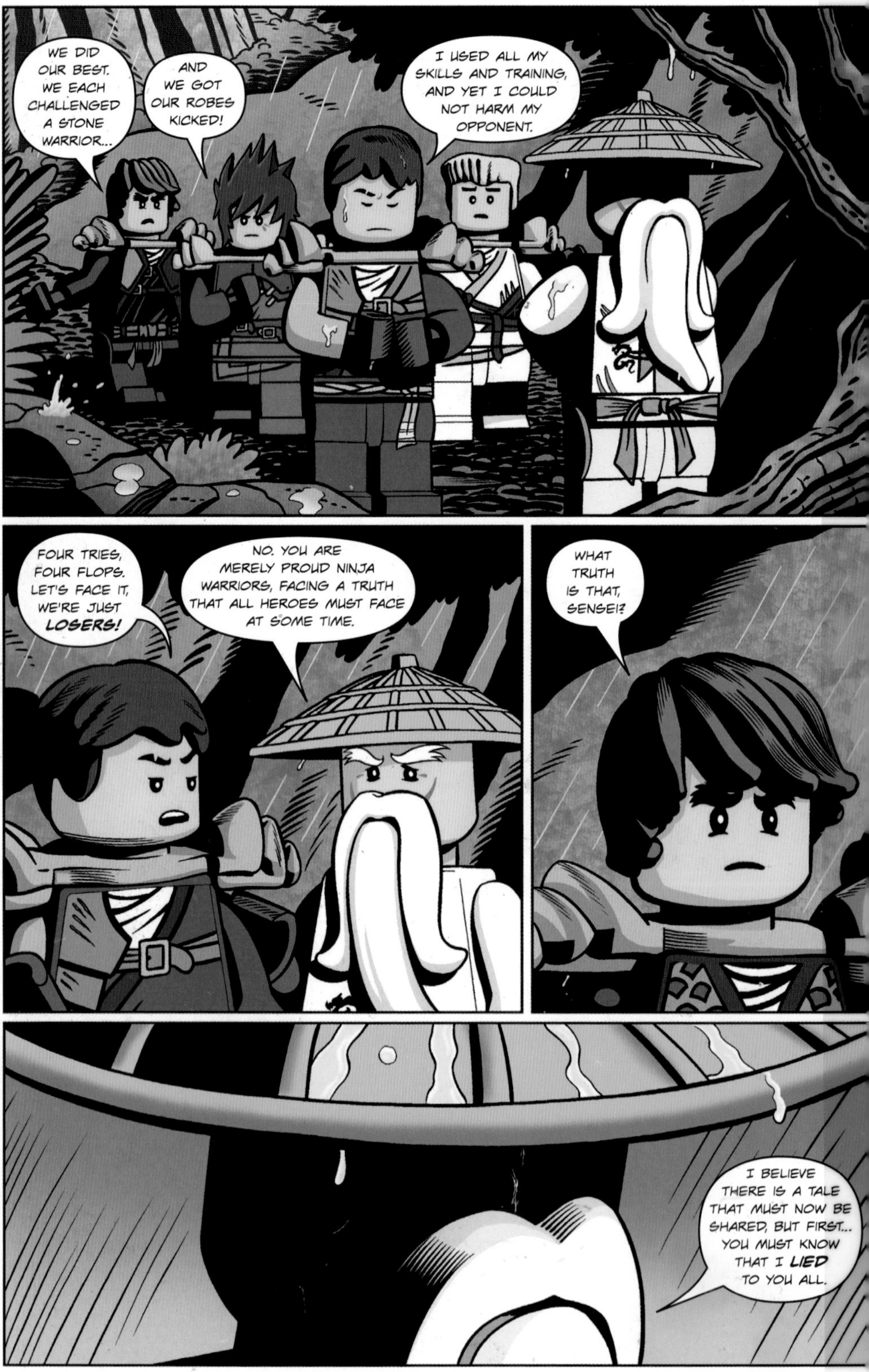
WE DID OUR BEST. WE EACH CHALLENGED A STONE WARRIOR...
AND WE GOT OUR ROBES KICKED!
I USED ALL MY SKILLS AND TRAINING, AND YET I COULD NOT HARM MY OPPONENT.
FOUR TRIES, FOUR FLOPS. LET'S FACE IT, WE'RE JUST **LOSERS!**
NO. YOU ARE MERELY PROUD NINJA WARRIORS, FACING A TRUTH THAT ALL HEROES MUST FACE AT SOME TIME.
WHAT TRUTH IS THAT, SENSEI?
I BELIEVE THERE IS A TALE THAT MUST NOW BE SHARED, BUT FIRST... YOU MUST KNOW THAT I **LIED** TO YOU ALL.

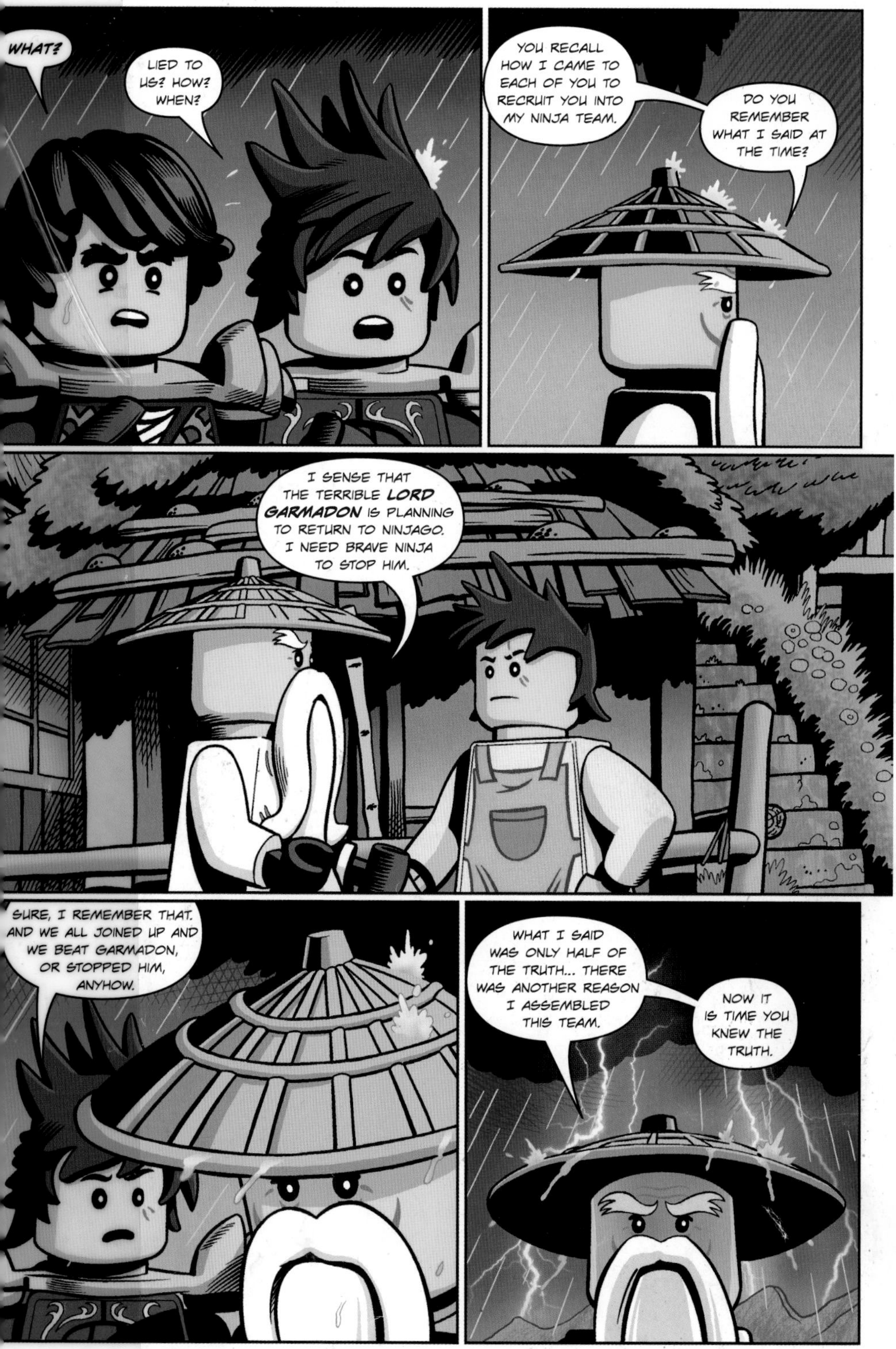
WHAT?
LIED TO US? HOW? WHEN?
YOU RECALL HOW I CAME TO EACH OF YOU TO RECRUIT YOU INTO MY NINJA TEAM.
DO YOU REMEMBER WHAT I SAID AT THE TIME?
I SENSE THAT THE TERRIBLE LORD GARMADON IS PLANNING TO RETURN TO NINJAGO. I NEED BRAVE NINJA TO STOP HIM.
SURE, I REMEMBER THAT. AND WE ALL JOINED UP AND WE BEAT GARMADON, OR STOPPED HIM, ANYHOW.
WHAT I SAID WAS ONLY HALF OF THE TRUTH... THERE WAS ANOTHER REASON I ASSEMBLED THIS TEAM.
NOW IT IS TIME YOU KNEW THE TRUTH.

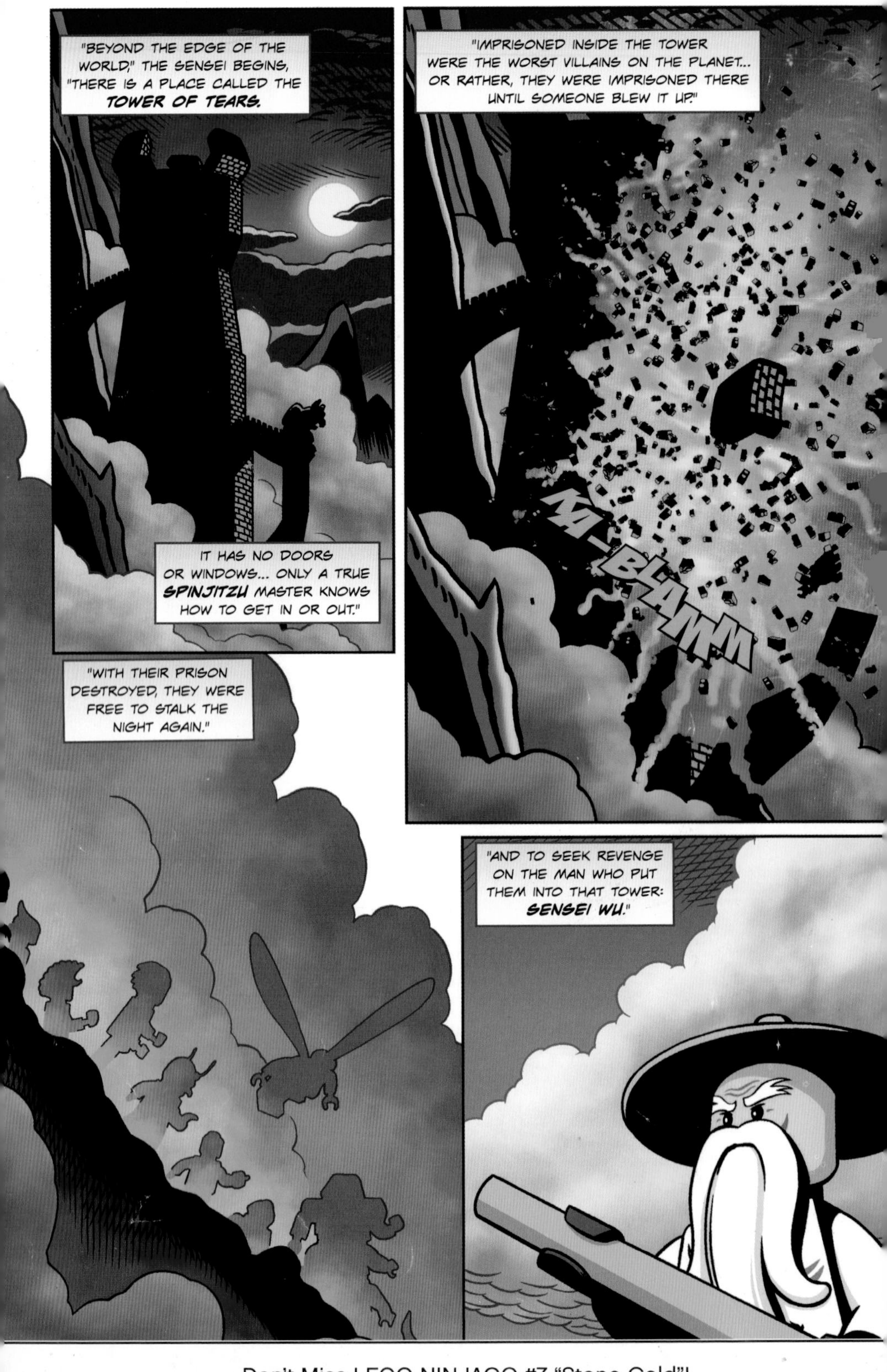
"BEYOND THE EDGE OF THE WORLD," THE SENSEI BEGINS, "THERE IS A PLACE CALLED THE **TOWER OF TEARS.**
IT HAS NO DOORS OR WINDOWS... ONLY A TRUE **SPINJITZU** MASTER KNOWS HOW TO GET IN OR OUT."
"IMPRISONED INSIDE THE TOWER WERE THE WORST VILLAINS ON THE PLANET... OR RATHER, THEY WERE IMPRISONED THERE UNTIL SOMEONE BLEW IT UP."
KA-BLAMMM
"WITH THEIR PRISON DESTROYED, THEY WERE FREE TO STALK THE NIGHT AGAIN."
"AND TO SEEK REVENGE ON THE MAN WHO PUT THEM INTO THAT TOWER: **SENSEI WU**."

Don't Miss LEGO NINJAGO #7 "Stone Cold"!

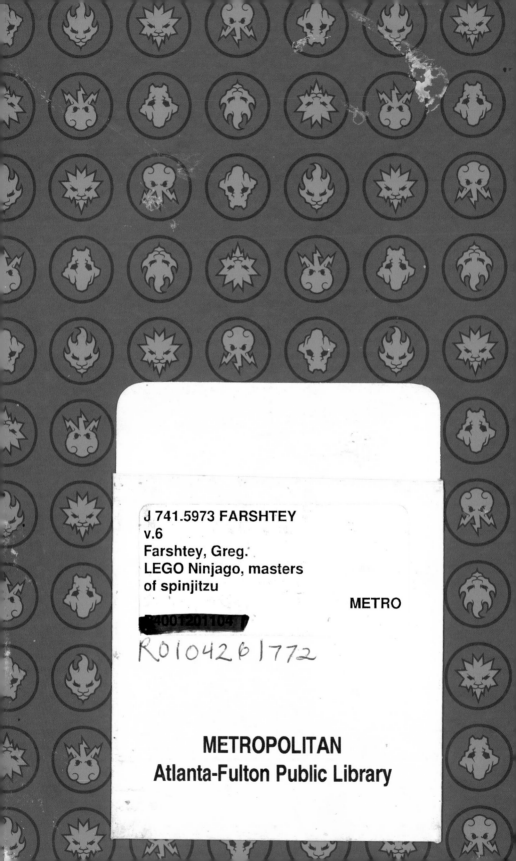